STATE OF GUILT

STATE OF GUILT

Johannes Kerkhoven

AuthorHouse™ UK Ltd.
500 Avebury Boulevard
Central Milton Keynes, MK9 2BE
www.authorhouse.co.uk
Phone: 08001974150

© 2010 Johannes Kerkhoven. All rights reserved.

No part of this book may be reproduced, stored in a retrieval system, or transmitted by any means without the written permission of the author.

First published by AuthorHouse 10/25/2010

ISBN: 978-1-4520-8419-0 (sc)

This book is printed on acid-free paper.

ABOUT THE AUTHOR

Johannes Kerkhoven, born in Holland, lived in Australia and now lives in London.

He obtained a B.A. in English in 2002 from Birkbeck College University of London.

His short stories and poetry have appeared in magazines and anthologies.

He co-authored Splinters of Light, a volume of poetry, published 2004 in the U.K.; U.S. Edition 2009.

In 2006 Hearing Eye published his collection of visual Poetry Mixed Concrete.

DEDICATION:

To my Family

PREFACE:

I was nine years old in 1940. It was later on during the war that German soldiers would invade our houses as they do in the novel. They were looking for able-bodied men, Jewish people, and towards the end, metals such as brass and copper for the weapons factories. It seems incomprehensible now, but my father would disappear into a space he had dug under the floor of our backroom, to escape being arrested.

My war experiences have already prompted me to write several short stories, but in this novel I have probably drawn on the last of my memories of the period.

Johannes Kerkhoven 2010

ACKNOWLEDGMENTS

First of all I owe a debt to Cristina, my partner of over twenty years, for her good-humoured patience and encouragement.

To the many friends who have read the manuscript of the novel I wish to express my thanks. Their valued comments have influenced my thinking. One of the first was the late William Hall, the biographer, who sadly will not see the finished product. Jeannie Hall I thank for using her considerable skills to spot and correct my sometimes clumsy phrasing and Dorothy Pope for proofreading the final manuscript

My gratitude to the eminent Dutch lawyer Mr. T. B. Boone, who generously answered my legal questions relating to Dutch Law, which gave the pertinent chapters a sense of authenticity.

Photograph of author on back cover by Lucienne Hodgson.

CHAPTER ONE

We had survived another day; one day closer to the capitulation of the mighty German Reich.

Mum had traded *Genesis* to *The Songs of Solomon* for a quantity of dried apple slices. The thin pages of her small bible were a perfect substitute for unobtainable cigarette papers.

The apple slices were now the only food in the house. 'Everyone take four each.'

After we had all put a hand into the bowl, she covered it with a tea towel.

We heard trucks and Mum sighed, 'Not again,' as Dad disappeared.

Ten or so German soldiers were jumping out of the trucks at the end of our street. They always did this when staging a razzia. The first thing would be to set up a machine gun at each end of the street and we could hear the truck going past our house and stopping again. Escape routes blocked, we waited our turn as the Germans entered each house. If your door was not opened promptly when they knocked with their rifle butts, they kicked it in.

Why had they come to our little street? Had someone been betrayed or were they looking for able-bodied men to send to Germany for slave-labour, Jews, members of the Resistance or did they merely want blankets or food?

Dad was arrested during one of the periodic round-ups of men. His arthritic hip which normally he could cope with, became his possible means of escape. He began to limp and his face showed such pain that the doctor who checked the prisoners gave him papers attesting that Mr van Land was unfit for all work. However, papers can be and often were torn up. To avoid being re-arrested he had dug himself a hiding place under the floor of the back room.

The makeshift cellar had a trap door usually covered by a rug. Below it was a space of about one by two and a half metres wide and about one and a half metres deep, with a canvas camp bed in it, a candle, the illegal radio receiver and some reading matter that felt and smelled moist. When we heard the soldiers Dad disappeared into "the hole", as we called it, in a flash. It was tolerable to be in that damp and musty place for half an hour, not much more.

Our house was halfway down the street and we waited as the soldiers worked their way towards us. We could hear shouting and the yelling of commands before the clattering of boots came down the cement path leading to our back door.

He was alone and young, not much older than I and certainly no bigger. He scowled at us. The steel helmet covered most of his head. He had a pointed pimply face and pale grey eyes that darted around our kitchen. I could see that the rifle he was carrying was too heavy for him as he pulled at the strap when it kept slipping down.

Mum stepped forward, bare arms on her hips, lips pressed together and bright blue eyes flashing.

The German ignored her, went into the living room and looked around as if he owned our house. We held our breath. Catching sight of the covered bowl on the sideboard he walked across letting the rifle slide into his hands. Mum, solid as a rock, was at once between him and our dried apple slices. The soldier holding his rifle with both hands pushed it roughly into her, his eyes never leaving the bowl. Mum stumbled and fell against the sideboard, letting out a sharp cry.

He had his back to me and without thinking I got my left arm around his throat and clamped my right one on the rim of his helmet and yanked it towards me. My knee was up the small of his back, and he came down, rifle and all. Albert and I each held an arm. Tina, my younger sister, sat on his legs. We yelled at him as he struggled.

Mum was back on her feet. 'Hands off our food!' she spat at him, jabbing a finger close to his eyes.

He looked up at her, shaking. You could almost hear him thinking: *This is not supposed to happen. I'm the Übermensch here,* but he nodded as if he understood. He glanced at his rifle on the floor next to him and I kicked it away.

Mum threw up her arms and said, 'Oh, God, what now?'

Unable to answer, we looked at her expectantly.

'Dad,' Mum called out.

He had come out of the hiding place and came into the room, alarm in his voice, 'What's all the commotion?'

He saw the soldier on the floor. 'What have you done? We'll all be shot!'

'He pushed Mum,' I said.

'Yes,' Mum was very angry, 'he was going to steal our apple slices.'

Dad's expression hardened. 'The big soldiers are pushing women around are they?' He looked down at the cringing boy on the floor with such anger that I could see he wanted to kill him there and then and might have done so if he had been alone with him.

Although there was shouting outside, no more soldiers came in.

Dad pulled the helmet off the soldier's head, picked up the rifle and took the big bayonet from the belt around the German's waist.

Without his helmet he looked small. Dad towered over him.

'He's only a boy,' Mum said. I expected her to slap the German's face.

'Maybe so but he's as dangerous as any of them,' Dad answered. 'He'd kill us all if we gave him the chance.'

We were holding onto the soldier, waiting for Dad's next move and only let go as he pointed the rifle at the boy. 'Get up.'

'What are we going to do with him?' Mum asked, her voice shaking.

'His friends are still all over the street,' Dad said. 'If they miss him – ,' he shook his head. 'No, I don't want to think about that. First I'll get him out of sight into the hole and keep him quiet.'

The soldier had let out one cry, which I had cut short by putting my hand over his mouth. I rubbed my hands

State of Guilt

together drying his spit and my sweat. He didn't take his eyes off Dad, who was holding his rifle and bayonet.

'Go on!'

He pushed the soldier to the hiding place and motioned for him to get in. Dad handed the rifle to me and followed him in. I lowered the heavy gun into Dad's waiting hands and we closed the trapdoor after them. Mum straightened the rug over it and we waited in the kitchen. Mum had her arms around Albert and Tina. Would Dad have his hands around the German's throat or the bayonet pushed against his ribs? I pictured the bayonet going right through the soldier's puny body, pinning him to the earthen walls the same way we pin notes to our kitchen door.

Nobody spoke. Outside it became quiet. 'The soldiers must have got to the end of the street,' I thought. 'They will miss him now and come storming back into the houses, screaming and swearing.' We stayed very still, Mum's face white against her black hair.

Truck engines started up and, after roaring loudly, faded away. Could the soldiers be driving off without the one in our cellar? It didn't seem possible; they must have realised that one of their group was missing. I heard Rose, Anja's mother, yell something in her garden next door, probably sending a series of curses after the Germans.

We did not move. At last Mum said. 'Have they gone? It might be a trick. Piet, go and look outside to make sure.'

The street was empty. Several front doors opened and shut again as our neighbours also made certain the Germans had gone.

They had left and we all breathed deeply.

'Thank you, God,' Mum said, closing her eyes for a

second. She went into the back room, pulled the rug away from the trap-door and opened it.

'They've gone. They've forgotten him,' she said, elbows close to her side, her body looked tense.

Dad blinked as he came out. The soldier grabbed his leg wanting to follow him. Dad handed the rifle to me and half turning showed the bare bayonet to the German, who then let go.

Dad closed the trap-door and said. 'They may have gone, but we'll leave him in there for the moment. I'll go over to Johan Bakker tonight after dark. He and I can decide what will happen to the soldier.'

A printer by profession, Dad hadn't worked for some months as nearly all commercial activity had ceased. He and Mr Bakker produced a free mini-newspaper on a hidden printing press which gave information about the war. Bakker, who was a journalist, gathered the news from his connections with the Resistance. I was given the job of distributing these illegal leaflets a few times and felt proud doing it and tried not to think that it also terrified me because of what would happen if I was caught.

'What can Bakker do?' Mum asked, not happy about Dad going out.

She had good reason I thought, remembering that Anja's father was shot as he rushed to his home next to ours, during curfew.

Dad disagreed; he meant to do what he thought best. 'Bakker will find out what can be done and don't worry, I'll creep through the alleys; no one will see me. We know German soldiers are held as prisoners of war somewhere. This boy is not going to be kept locked up here, is he, or else …'

State of Guilt

'What else?' Mum pressed him.

'Well, what do we do, starve him to death or let him take food away from us? We have nothing to give him and we can't let him go. He'd be back soon enough with the whole German army and the Gestapo; they'd enjoy shooting all of us.'

'You can't let them kill him. He's so young.'

Dad shrugged his shoulders and showed his palms. 'Remember, he's old enough to shoot us.'

While we were discussing the soldier's future, he began to call out and bang on the trap door, perhaps thinking his comrades might hear and he would be rescued.

Dad stood up, 'Let's hope he will be written off as one more deserter. The war is no longer going their way. The Germans are starting to panic. We'll be free within days; I know it!'

We followed him into the back room. By then the soldier was almost out of the hiding place. He stopped as he saw us looking down at him, his own naked bayonet, immense in Dad's steady hand, pointed straight at him.

'If you give us trouble …' Dad slowly drew the long steel blade across his own throat, his eyes hard, locked on to the soldier's fear-filled face. The boy soldier took his time, closing the trap door over his head.

Before all the schools had been closed because there was no heating, I had finished two years of high school and had been taught German, French and English while during the five years of German occupation, I had picked up quite a bit more of the language.

Dad told me to explain the position to him. 'And see what you can find out about his unit. Are they planning to move out soon? Tell that boy that he must not make any noise. Pile it on a bit. Make it sound as bad as you can. If he screams in German, one of those traitors walking past the house might hear him.'

Either of the two collaborators who lived in our street, would happily inform the Germans if they had any suspicions. That is, if they had not left for Germany, as many of them had already done, thinking they would be safe there. They knew what would happen to them if they were around on liberation day.

I went into the hiding place and found it unpleasantly damp, the soldier stank of sweat. As best as I could, I told him. 'If we let you go, you will be back with half your army and shoot us all so we can't do that.'

'Ach, nein!' he said with conviction. 'I would not!'

I laughed, 'Who believes that, deserves to die. If you feel generous, you'll shoot my father and have the rest of us carted off to a concentration camp.'

'Nein, nein!' he shook his head vigorously. 'Let me go, and I will never come back.'

Looking at him by the light of one of our last stumpy candles I went on, 'We could hand you over to the Resistance. Of course, we can't keep you. We could kill you ourselves. We'll bury you in our garden and grow tomatoes on top of you.'

He grabbed my hand, sweat running down his cheeks. His mouth was open, his bottom lip trembling. 'I didn't mean to push your mother. It was wrong of me. *Ich bitte vielmals um Entschuldigung!* I'm very sorry.'

I pulled free from his sweaty grip, 'If we thought you would do as we ask, we could put in a good word for you and tell the Resistance that you are a good German.'

He blinked rapidly, eyelids fluttering. I could see he

was fighting back tears and I felt disgusted. What sort of a soldier was he? Not so brave now without his rifle as he had been when he pushed his way into our house. I also felt slightly awkward and embarrassed.

'What's your name?' I pretended to be interested. Maybe it would calm him a little.

'Kurt, Kurt Grutz.'

'Well, Kurt Grutz, you must be very quiet or you will make things difficult for us, but even more so for yourself. Remember that.'

He nodded.

'How long have you been a soldier, Kurt?'

'Three months, only three months. I never wanted to be a soldier. I don't like it. I want to go home.'

'Is the German army going back to Germany soon? Have they told you anything?'

'Nothing. They tell us nothing. All we do is exercise.'

'And raid Dutch homes,' I said.

He shook his head. 'None of us want to do it; we want to go home. It's the officers that make us do these things. We have to follow orders. If we don't, they shoot us.'

It was obvious that if he knew anything he wasn't going to tell. The Resistance might find out more.

'We're not having him here more than one day,' Dad said, 'and I won't have you give him any food, not a scrap. He probably had pork chops for lunch so going without food for a few hours won't kill him.'

I tried to remember what pork chops tasted like but I kept thinking of the sugar beet cakes Mum made every day. So I said, 'He might have had roast beef with big snow-white potatoes and peas and green beans and lots

Johannes Kerkhoven

of gravy all over all of it.' That I could imagine and my mouth watered so much I had to swallow.

It made everybody laugh. 'No more of that, Piet. Stop it.'

Mum decided it wasn't human to keep him in the hiding place. 'It's too damp down there, Dad. Every time you come out of that hole you're all shivery. He could die down there.'

I thought, well, Dad has to go in there every time those bloody Germans come anywhere near our street, so what's the problem? I'd tie him up and push one of his own dirty socks down his Kraut throat to keep him quiet. If he died, well, we hadn't asked him to come into our house. It was decided that we would lock him in the top bedroom at the back of the house. That was my bedroom. It meant I had to sleep on the floor in the back room downstairs.

'It's only going to be for one night,' Dad said. He was angry.

So was I.

'Once he's gone, you'll have clean sheets again,' Mum said to me.

Our house was two storeys high and Dad had converted part of the loft into a bedroom for me and had fitted a small skylight into the roof. There was a strong lock on my bedroom door, and the skylight was minute and high up so we felt that Kurt would not be able to get out, and we had impressed on him that if he called out, he would die before us.

Dad instructed me to tell him again that he'd better behave. I wanted to go up with him for a while anyway. I didn't want him going through my things. I intended to lock most of my possessions in the wardrobe.

I asked him where he came from and got out my atlas.

'Münster. I live in Münster.'

'That's not very far from our border. Perhaps when the war is over, I'll come and visit you.' I don't know why I said that; I intended never to set foot in Germany.

Talking to this slight, mousy-haired boy, I felt an odd mixture of power, distaste and pity. He was our prisoner, and we were in charge, yet he would attack us if given the chance. It was like pinning down a poisonous snake with a forked stick, just behind its head. It can't bite you like that. However, if you let go, watch out.

Kurt showed me some pictures of his parents and sister – a chubby dark-haired girl of about twelve, with a button for a nose and a disgustingly plump body. It seemed strange to me that a German soldier could be part of a ruthless killing force and at the same time of a family, doing the things we did, like having meals together or celebrating birthdays. Could they have feelings of love for anyone, when they had made killing their profession?

'My father was a soldier too. He was an officer, a captain.'

'Was?' I said.

'Yes. He died in Russia.' He said it as if he were saying, 'Today is Friday.'

I imagined what I would feel if Dad were to die, and remembered how Anja had not left her house for a week after her father had been shot. I found it impossible to understand how anyone could talk about his father the way this boy did but then, he was a soldier. He might even have killed people, maybe people like us. I imagined him and his sister in the *Hitler Jugend*. It made me shiver and stopped me from feeling too friendly towards him.

That night Albert and I went into the back garden when we heard the nightly drone of planes. The bombers flew high up over Holland, making their way through the puffs of ack-ack, like great ships, sailing through the sky on their way to their German targets.

Albert grabbed my arm and I froze as one of the planes was snared by the searchlights. The guns were sending up shells at a tremendous rate. One of the engines caught fire and the plane started to lose height. The needles of light locked onto it, chasing it down. Lower and lower it came then went into a dive, a thick black trail of smoke behind it. Its remaining engines screamed, trying to the last to save the great machine. A bright flash and seconds later the sound of an explosion told us that the plane had been destroyed on impact and that the men in it must have died. I hoped some had escaped by parachute. The rest of the airborne armada droned on. We listened without speaking until we could no longer hear them.

Later that night when Dad came back from seeing Mr Bakker, he told us that the German would be moved the next day. He led us in a prayer for a quick end to the war and for the crew of the plane that had been shot down and for their families.

My friend Jan had seen the plane fall too and we talked about it the next day.

'One airman came down and his parachute didn't open,' Jan said. 'He jammed up to his waist into the wet ground and had a half-smoked cigar clenched between his teeth.'

CHAPTER TWO

From the front room came the murmur of voices. I listened to what sounded like Mr. Bakker, then Dad and Mum. I lifted a corner of the curtain. The sky was ash-grey. Not quite daylight yet.

I got up, put on my shirt and trousers and went into the passage to better hear what was being said. After all, I should know what was going on. Were they about to take the German soldier away?

Mr. Bakker said, 'No, there's no point in meeting him now. I must run. I'll send one of the children over as soon as I know something.'

'As long as it's today,' Dad answered.

'That's understood.'

They came out of the room. Mr Bakker looked surprised to see me. He only said, 'Hello Piet,' as he walked through the kitchen and out of the back door.

'What's happening, Dad?'

The lines around his eyes were deeper than usual. He looked as if he had not slept enough. 'We're going to have to look after our German for a few more hours. Let's hope we won't have another raid before we get rid of him. Mr Bakker's contacts promised that arrangements will be made for taking the German off our hands. That's all.'

'What will happen to him?' Mum's voice was flat, without emotion. I felt that she would no longer object to whatever was going to be done. I was glad.

'What will happen to him?' Dad rubbed his chin and shrugged. 'We'll have to wait and see, won't we. It's not up to me.' He looked grim. 'They'll come and pick him up from here. If not, well, it's only a five minute walk to Bakker's house through the alleyways. He and I can walk him over. The boy will wear my overcoat, that'll come down to his ankles. No one will think there's a soldier of the Reich under there. I think he's scared enough to behave himself. If he becomes difficult – well, we can always dig a hole for him in the back garden.'

'Can we give him something to eat?' Mum asked softly.

'I thought we said no.'

'I've made some sugar beet cakes.'

Dad shook his head. The faintest of smiles crossed his face. 'You're incorrigible. One then, the smallest. I'll be surprised if he eats it. No reflection on your cooking, Mum.' He grinned and turned. 'Piet, go and bring him down.'

I glanced at Dad. He had picked up the bayonet and his knuckles were white. He looked determined. I thought he looked like a hero, and I was proud of him. I wondered if it had already been decided that the German would be killed and if Dad would have to do it. I knew he wouldn't tell us if that were so. All I knew was that right now the soldier was our responsibility. I shivered a little. I had

State of Guilt

begun to think of him as Kurt. He had a name now but he was still the enemy. It was still him or us.

It was dangerous and exciting to have a prisoner. We were in control. It felt as if we were winning the war. We needed to hold on a bit longer. This time the Allies were really close, not like the disaster of last year when they landed at Arnhem.

I hoped they might decide not to kill him or if they did that it would not be Dad who would have to do it.

I turned the key to my bedroom door.

'Gute Morgen,' I started to say cheerfully. The last syllable never came out. The bed was empty, it had been dragged underneath the skylight and the chair was lying on top of it. I whirled around, panic overtaking me. 'Dad! He's not here!' I yelled down the staircase. 'He's gone!'

'No!' Dad came bounding up the stairs. 'He can't be.'

He looked under the bed and pulled out the metal-tipped army boots from underneath. He yanked the crumpled blankets off the bed. There was no possible hiding place in my small room.

I felt icy cold. 'What now?' We would have to act fast. Who knows how long Kurt had been gone. 'You must leave at once, Dad.' I had visions of the soldiers dragging him away and could almost hear the sirens and the scream of tyres as trucks raced towards our house.

'Yes, but how? How did he get out?' He was still holding the bayonet but his hand was no longer steady.

'Over the roof?' I pointed at the chair on my bed under the open skylight. 'He must have got out there. But it's so small.'

Dad shook his head in disbelief. His Adam's apple

bobbed up and down as he swallowed. 'How could he – ?' He shook his head. 'I don't want to believe it yet it's the only answer. He managed to get out onto the roof and then down. He must be made of rubber.'

'Please go now, Dad.'

'You'd better get out, too,' Dad said, resolute again. 'In fact we'd all better be gone. There's no telling what they'll do. Come on, this time they'll come only for us and they will be very happy to finish us all off.'

I took my big knife out of the wardrobe. Until now it had only been used for whittling and cutting up fruit. I'd never thought of it as a weapon. I put it on my belt. It wasn't as big as a bayonet, but it felt good. If necessary I would use it. I imagined the hole I would make in a German uniform. My blade would glide in as it would into butter.

Mum was in the kitchen. Dad called Albert and Tina and quickly explained what had happened.

Tina began to cry and Albert looked as if he was about to cry too. Mum let out the only swear word I had ever known her to use. 'Verdomme! I should have listened to you. If we'd kept him under the floor …'

'Never mind that,' Dad said. 'I should have made sure that he could not get out, tied him up, anything. It's done now so let's make sure we get out of here quickly.'

We all grabbed our coats. Dad hid the German rifle under his long coat. Mum and Dad kissed. He pressed her against his chest for a second or two and said, 'I'll go to Bakker's house. His hiding place is big enough for the two of us if we need to disappear. Of course we can't all go there. We must split up.'

Mum nodded. 'We can go to Mrs. de Vries. Here everyone, take some more dried apple slices.'

'Quickly now,' Dad said. 'Piet, you go over to Nick's place and watch our house from there.'

Nick was one of my school friends, who lived farther down the street. From his house I would be able to see whatever went on.

'Go now,' Mum said.

Dad kissed each of us on the cheek. 'Stop crying,' he hugged Tina. 'They haven't got us yet.' Then he was gone. We all left the house and I could see him hurrying out into the alley.

I felt responsible. I would make certain that Mum, Albert and Tina would get safely to Mrs. de Vries. If there was any trouble – I patted my knife for reassurance.

CHAPTER THREE

When I had delivered Mum, Albert and Tina to Mrs. de Vries's, I thought I could spend some time with Anja. I would be safe there. I went back to our street keeping to the alleys. They ran between the houses in our neighbourhood and I knew them like I knew the down on my upper lip. One of the high wooden fences bore traces of a chalk-drawn target that we had used for knife-throwing practice. A little further on was the brick wall where we used to stage our high peeing contests.

I had to get back to our street. Every so often I stopped and listened for truck engines.

It was full daylight and the sun was half-heartedly working its way through the thin, light grey cover of clouds. I looked both ways as I went to cross Egmont Street to disappear quietly out of sight again down the alley opposite.

Without warning, a tall skinny old man came running towards me from nowhere. His eyes glittered madly and his arms flailed in the air. Before I could evade him, he had grabbed me and his fingers were digging hard into my

State of Guilt

arm. He swung me round with unbelievable strength in a wild dance. My God, had he gone mad with hunger? My legs panicked and dangled behind me like slack ropes.

He was yelling hysterically at the top of his shrill old voice. 'Yooohoooo! It's over, it's over, the war is over, it's over, ove-e-er. I heard it on the radio. The bastards have surrendered!'

Could it be? One minute there was nobody to be seen, the next, as if by magic, the street was full of people and I knew the old man was right. I was dragged along, yelling with them, going round and round with the old man and others joining us, dancing, jumping and yelling. I felt dizzy with exhilaration. More and more people were streaming onto the streets, hundreds of them, filling the air with their shouts and laughter.

The feeling of relief was so great in everyone that, in an instant, it was as if we had all become part of one consciousness. No matter who you looked at, friends, acquaintances and strangers alike, their eyes alight, the whole nation was deliriously happy. The first day of the new world had begun.

Anja! It flashed through my head. I must get to her and the others, all of us safe now. Dad and Mum might be on their way home.

I pulled away and stopped the old man. I kissed him on both sunken, stubbly cheeks. His pale shining eyes were beautiful. I could smell strong stale sweat, but I loved him. 'Must go home.' I cupped my hand over his hairy ear to make him hear me.

He nodded brightly, wiped the tears of happiness from his eyes and let go of me. He looked at me for a moment, then turned towards the crowd. As I walked away he had already grabbed a young woman around the waist. She laughed and put her arms around him as they waltzed away.

I laughed wildly and ran up our alley to get to the back of the house. We always kept a key to the back door hidden under a stone. You could hear people yelling in the streets and I again laughed out loud with happiness as I stood there listening. Everybody was going berserk. My God. I breathed in deeply. We would never have to be afraid again, not ever, and there would be enough to eat for everybody, always. There would be warm clothes and new bicycles and cars in the streets without those silly gas bags on top. There would be school again. I even looked forward to that. So many things went through my head. Happiness was almost bursting out of me. I could have flown up into the blue sky. I knew that I would never ever have a day like this again if I lived ten thousand years.

Anja and I had an agreement that if I whistled the first five notes of a song we both knew, it meant I was waiting for her outside. I whistled my signal.

CHAPTER FOUR

Piet! Bitte ...'
I turned around sharply.

'Kurt!' Instantly my elation was gone and my hand was on my knife. I was shaking. For a split second it was war again and I was confronted by a German soldier. What was he doing here? He had been wiped from my world. My head was too full of the new, free life that had started. There was no room for him in my mind.

He looked terrified and his white face was streaked with blood and mud. His uniform was dirty and torn and he had no boots on. They were still upstairs in my bedroom. I saw he was shaking more than I was and I recovered. The war was over and there was no need for us to be afraid any more, not ever again. It was time now for the Germans and the traitors to be afraid.

'What ...?' I started but he did not have to answer.

Any German seen on our streets that day would be killed. I did not doubt that. We had suffered too much. Kurt had been lucky that he had not been caught. I said it in my head loud and clear, "We are free. All of us." It felt good, so good that I didn't need to feel a scrap of hatred for him. He looked funny and stupid, vulnerable and very scared like a child. What had happened to him? He must have been on his way back to his barracks, I thought, and he would have been too late. The news of the liberation had broken and at that same moment his life was in danger. He had come back to our house in desperation.

I heard a different kind of yelling, not the deliriously happy sounds that came from the streets. It was closer and, yes, excited. This was ugly, raw and threatening, screaming and swearing and suddenly there was a loud bang as a gun was fired. These were people out for deadly revenge, revenge for the years of occupation, hunger, and worse still, the torture and the murders. Could they be after Kurt?

'Quick, into the shed, behind the wood.' I opened the door as fast as I could.

They came running. Six of them, yelling and pushing each other to speed up their chase through the narrow alley. They saw me and stopped. The first one, a big man with short grey hair dressed in a blue overall, came half way into our garden. He glared at me and waved his pistol at me. I stood with my back against the door of the shed.

'Hey you! Where is he!? Did you see the Kraut?'

The man scared me and I couldn't speak. I only managed to nod and point in the direction of the Olden Lane, the street that ran along the far end of our block.

They all yelled at once. 'Let's go. Get him. Yes, get the Kraut, then the traitors!' They were gone.

I was about to go into the shed when the gate swung open again. It was Albert. He ran up to me.

'You've got to come to Mrs de Vries. We're all there, Piet. It's a big party, with food. Bread and butter. Everyone has brought something to eat. And,' he laughed, 'and I had a glass of milk!'

'Milk?' I licked my lips. 'All right, I'll be along in a minute.'

I had to hide Kurt first. Albert stood waiting for me, small and skinny. 'Go on.' I said. 'You go back and tell Mum I'm coming.'

He stood there, probably wondering why I didn't want to come at once. I took a threatening step towards him, and he looked at Anja's house and ran off laughing as if he understood. 'Bread and butter,' he called out.

Kurt was cowering in the shadowy corner of the shed. He trembled uncontrollably and the whites of his eyes were immense.

'Bitte, bitte,' he kept whimpering, and he stood up, clinging to me.

His sharp body odour overwhelmed the smell of the chopped pine wood that filled the corner of the shed. I pushed him away. 'Don't do that.'

I couldn't leave him in the shed. Dad and the others would come home after the party, maybe sooner. We would have to hand him over to someone. To that mob? I couldn't do that. Today was a happy day. I didn't want any hate or killing. We needed time. He would not stand a chance anywhere on the street. Everyone had gone mad. Reason had taken the day off. Maybe tonight or tomorrow.

Quite calm now, I knew what had to be done.

'You must take off your uniform. I will get you some clothes. I'll be back soon.'

Johannes Kerkhoven

I went inside and up the stairs to my room and took out some of my older clothes.

Back in the shed I thrust them at him. 'Here, put these on.'

He looked ridiculous in his dirty underwear. He'd been crying and I could see that he had peed himself. Any other time I would have burst out laughing. Now I felt sorry for him although not too much. I never liked cry-babies and after all he was still a German.

'Danke, danke, danke,' he kept repeating as if he were a toddler who had learned his first word. He put his army trousers on the floor and thrust a wallet into my hand.

'If anything happens to me, please post this to my mother.'

I put it in my pocket and nodded as he put his skinny white legs into my old trousers. 'Please hurry.'

My clothes fitted him near enough. I couldn't worry about the fact that Mum would miss them, not now. I stuffed his uniform behind the wood pile.

There was one place where he would be safe for a while: the bombed house where Anja and I had our secret meeting place.

I coaxed Kurt out of the shed and we ran along the back alley. A minute later we were in the little cellar. The slit above the small door let in a little light. I motioned to him to sit on the makeshift bench I had made.

'I will bring you some food and drink,' I said.

He nodded, still shaking and again began his monotonous, *'Danke, danke, danke.'*

'Eine Stunde. One hour,' I told him. I would have to go to the party at Mrs. de Vries's for a while or I would be missed and someone might come looking for me.

I ran through the alleys as much as possible because the streets were full of people: dense crowds, dancing, yelling, laughing or crying.

'Piet, you look so serious,' someone yelled at me and was carried past me by the crowd before I could answer.

I had to force a smile then the thought of the German I'd hidden took my happiness away. Could I tell Dad? Maybe I'll tell him tonight when we are alone. He'll know what to do without Kurt getting hurt.

There was another shot. It was the men I'd sent away earlier. They were looking down an alley, waving their guns. I didn't want them to see me and managed to reach the end of the street while they argued.

Seeing those men again made me want to hurry. That was difficult. I had to stop several times and join in the singing of our national anthem: *'Wilhelmus'*. We sang it again at the party. My voice trembled a little when everyone smiled at me and probably thought I was too overcome with emotion, which I was.

Mr de Vries's house had already been decorated with streamers of orange coloured paper. There was food, bread, butter and dry biscuits that had been dropped to us from the air. A feast! Mr de Vries brought out some bottles of wine. They had lain under the floor of his kitchen during the whole of the war, quietly waiting for Liberation Day. Now we could drink a toast. 'Long live Queen Wilhelmina!'

It was decided that I was grown up enough to join in. So for the first time in my life I tasted wine. I could feel the effect and liked it.

CHAPTER FIVE

Liberation Day had turned into one big street party. Everyone danced and sang the songs that we had not been able to sing for so long.

'Piet Hein, Piet Hein, in stature he was klein, but his deeds were mighty tall.'

He was the admiral who was short and tied a broom to the mast of his ship to show how he had swept the sea clear of Holland's enemies.

Orange, our national colour, was everywhere. During the war bright orange marigolds had grown in many gardens, silently saying, 'We're not down yet.' Our red, white and blue flag was flying from most houses, some dusty or creased, no doubt the result of having been hidden for five long years in who knows what secret places. I thought that would make a good story. *Where we hid our flag.*

I had to go back to Kurt and I wanted to see Anja. After what seemed about half an hour at the party, I said that I would go and see my friend Nick.

State of Guilt

'All right,' Mum laughed, suddenly young. I had never seen her face beaming with such brightness.

I managed to wrap a few dry biscuits in my handkerchief, unused and clean that morning, and put the little parcel in my pocket for Kurt. I noticed his big German rifle in the corner behind Mr de Vries's chair.

I started to run to our house. I could feel and hear the milk and the wine I had drunk slosh around in my stomach. It made me feel nauseous, so I stopped running.

Our back door was unlocked. I'd forgotten to replace the key under the stone. I shrugged, would anybody be bothered to burgle today? As I came out of the back door, carrying a bottle of water for Kurt, Anja was outside in her garden. 'Blast,' I thought, 'This is the last thing I need.' I'd hoped I could attend to Kurt first.

'Hello, Anja,' I tried to sound casual. 'Isn't it wonderful to be free again?'

She didn't smile back. Why wasn't she happy? Was she still sad about her father? 'Is something wrong?'

'No.' She shook her head but pouted her lips and wrinkled her forehead. I could see that she was angry.

Their garden was a little higher than ours, and the sun, stronger now, was behind her and crowned her hair with a halo. She looked down on me like a goddess or like a saint who had just stepped out of a medieval painting. She wore the faded-blue sleeveless dress that I loved to see on her. Her slim round arms were folded across her chest.

'What have you been doing? I heard your whistle and expected you to be there waiting for me, then ...' I could feel ice in her voice, ice and steel.

'I ... we've been busy. I always have to cut the wood or there's nothing to cook on.'

'I know Piet. I know what you're up to,' she said without a hint of a smile. 'And I don't like it.'

'What do you mean?'

'Where are you going with that bottle of water? I saw you and that German. I heard you speak German to him. Where did you hide him? I also heard the men that were after him. You sent them the wrong way.'

I walked up to the dividing fence. 'It's not what you think, Anja. Please trust me. I had to send that mob away. They would have killed him there and then. I couldn't let that happen. The war is over now, for everybody. He's like us now.'

'You should trust me and not do things in secret. I saw you run off with him. You've given him some of your clothes.' The coldness in her voice made me feel utterly miserable. It was as if I was a stranger to her.

'So do we have to have secrets from each other? If I had only known you were a traitor and a friend of the Germans, I would never have spoken to you. I thought we ... you know, were going to be together always. How can I ever again be with you now?'

She was right. We were very close and I loved her so much. Besides, did I have any choice? I had to tell her.

'Do you remember the last lot of Germans that came yesterday?'

'Of course I do. Is it one of them? Did he desert? Then you should report him. You're hiding him, aren't you?' Her questions came quick and sharp.

'Nothing like that. He pushed Mum and she fell ... well, we threw him to the floor and sat on him. Dad came

State of Guilt

out of the hiding place and the soldier saw him. So we couldn't let him go, could we? We locked him up in my bedroom. He was our prisoner.'

'Your what?' Her eyes widened and I saw that her anger had instantly been replaced by excitement.

I pulled my shoulders back. 'Yes. It was all we could do. If we'd let him go then, he would have come back with the whole German army and we would all have been shot. But he escaped from my locked room. Then, when he realised the war was over, he knew he would be torn to pieces if he were caught. He came back to our house, hoping that we would protect him.

Her forehead wrinkled again. 'You've put him in our cellar in the bombed house, haven't you?'

I nodded. 'It was the only place I could think of.'

'Come inside, I'll give you some food,' she said.

I'd seen her mother in the street a little earlier. I felt embarrassed and uncomfortable about going into their house while Anja was there alone. I knew I was beginning to blush. 'I must take him some food and this water.' I held up the bottle.

'Come on, that can wait for a bit.' She was laughing at me now. 'Nobody's watching, or are you scared of me?'

I rolled my eyes, put the bottle down, jumped over the fence and followed her in.

Anja was two years older than me. It always felt good to be close to Anja. She was my best friend and someone to steal a kiss from. However this was different. I knew *it* was going to happen. I wanted it to happen so much, even if right now I could not get the German boy out of my head. Anja's eyes were determined.

'You won't tell anyone about the German?' I said.

She smiled and pulled me inside. Her lips were crushing mine while the click of the back door lock still hung in the air. 'Come upstairs into my room where we can talk,' she breathed into my ear and pulled me along, her hand cool over mine which was hot and very sweaty.

I could not think of anything to say. I also knew that my face was by now crimson. I hoped that in the subdued light she would not notice. Unbearably loud hammering inside my chest made me want to run away. I followed her up the steep stairs. I couldn't argue with her, not now, even while wanting her so badly, I must convince her that I had to protect Kurt. Anja mustn't tell anyone about Kurt.

She shut the bedroom door and drew the curtains. There was a thin strip of bright daylight on the ceiling. She pulled me against her and her soft warm lips were on mine again, her tongue darting into my mouth. Grabbing hold of my shirt collar, she undid the first few buttons, then, her breath quickening, she threw her arms wide and yanked the shirt open, ripping off the last three buttons. I could hear them rolling along the linoleum.

'Come on.' She tore at my bulging trousers, undoing the sterner buttons of my flies. With trembling fingers I helped her.

She pulled the dress up over her head and she was naked.

Kurt vanished from my thoughts.

She pulled me onto the bed. It was the very first time I felt all of her skin, warm and so smooth against mine. She began to kiss my neck and my chest and touched my nipples. I felt nerves tingle I did not know I had. I put my hands on her breasts and my cock became unbearably hard. I pushed it up against her stomach and then it was in her hand. She parted her legs and her hand guided me to the spot I had been dreaming about for so long. I slowly pushed inside her. She cried out as in if pain and took in a big gulp of air.

* * *

Anja was lying on top of me, her thick mass of blonde hair tickling my face. 'I knew it would be good. You're such a silly boy, aren't you? You're also my living teddy bear and I love you, even if you are a bit slow.'

'Much too slow.' I breathed in the faint smell of soap and of her heavenly body. It was almost too much. I felt great happiness. We've got rid of the Germans and Anja loves me. She is my woman now and at last I am a man.

'That was about time, Piet van Land. Now we have to make up for all the missed opportunities and all the fun we haven't had. We're both grown up now.'

Yes, I thought, no more boyish games. Was it already three years ago that I had shown Jan de Hout how to play with himself? No more of that silly handiwork. No more guilt and no more worry whether I'll lose the hair on my head and instead start to grow it on the palm of my hand.

My body had not stopped responding to Anja and holding her, I rolled over on top of her again.

She wriggled out from underneath me. 'Wait.' She got up off the bed, took a towel from the chest of drawers and wiped the blood from between her legs. She picked up her frock from the floor and put it on.

I watched in amazement. We'd only just begun. I wanted more.

Anja shook her head. 'Get dressed. I'll put on my

shoes in the kitchen. First I want you to take me to see your German. Then we'll do it again,' she laughed, 'as many times as you can do it.'

How many times would that be I wondered? I'd heard stories ... She was gone. By the time I had my trousers on and had walked down the steep stairs, I was limp and Kurt was back in my mind. Anja wanted to see him, but why now? I remembered then that I had to give him water and food. Better do it quickly. Anja will help me decide what we must do with him, who to tell. We couldn't very well have him living in that cellar forever.

Nobody saw us as we slipped along the back alley. Anja looked calm, very grown-up. Her clear blue eyes had a new brilliant glow in them. I felt it was the love-making. I had made her into a woman.

CHAPTER SIX

'Kurt, it's Piet.'

I held the door open for Anja and we went down the few steps into the cellar. My eyes took in the outline of her body and at once I could feel my own body responding. Later, I thought. I shook my head and turned to Kurt. 'Are you all right?'

He looked frightened and nodded.

'Here, I've brought you water.'

He closed his dirty fingers around the bottle and took a long drink. I placed the handkerchief with the biscuits on the little table and opened it, 'Something to eat.'

'Thank you.' Kurt looked at me and then at Anja.

'Don't worry. This is my friend, Anja,' I said. 'She knows about you.'

Kurt smiled a thin smile and held out his hand.

Anja smiled too, a fixed smile, and stepped towards him.

She did not take Kurt's hand. Instead she reached under her dress and in one continuous movement plunged an inch-wide blade deep into Kurt's chest.

It happened too fast for me to do anything. I screamed, 'No!' and grabbed at her arm.

She stepped back and turned to me, 'They killed my father.' Her voice was shaking and her eyes were pleading, desperately asking me to understand. 'Why should he live?'

Kurt's eyes were on me, huge, scared, begging. One arm made futile efforts to guide his fingers to the knife in his chest, the other reached out to me for help, *'Hilfe ...'*

His legs gave out and he crumpled to the floor.

I knelt beside him and supported his head. He let out a rasping sound, blood ran from his mouth, he sighed deeply and lay still. His eyes continued to stare at me and his hand clutched at my shirt.

He was dead, I knew. I trembled as I pulled his hand away from me. I let his head rest on the cellar floor and stared at Anja's white face, then back at the soldier and at Anja again, from one to the other, unable to believe what I had witnessed. The knife was stuck in his chest and I pulled it out and stood up, stunned.

'Don't Piet. Please don't look at me like that. I had to do it for my dad. They killed my dad and destroyed my mum. I had to do it. I had to do it. You understand that, don't you?'

Had this really happened? I couldn't move or speak. At the same time I wanted to scream at Anja, 'Take time back for two minutes and undo this.' My eyes again shifted from her face back to the dead soldier.

I became aware that I was still holding the knife. I looked at its bloody serrated edge and stretched my arm to hold it away.

Anja's eyes became softer, more like the eyes I knew,

as if she was coming out of a trance. She took the knife from my hand and let it drop to the floor.

She began to tremble uncontrollably and I could see the tears forming in her eyes. 'Hold me, Piet, hold me,' her voice barely audible.

As I held her, and maybe because of that, I calmed down somewhat. What could we do now? Kurt was lying dead at our feet. Nobody and nothing could change that.

I felt her grief and touched her face. 'Anja, my Anja.'

'Oh, Piet, I ... I thought that this soldier might be one of the men who laughed while they shot my father.' She swallowed hard. 'You see that I had to do it. I saw my dad after ... I can still see him. I'll never forget, never. When you told me about this German I knew that I would kill the murderer. So I took Dad's knife out of his fishing bag. I've taken revenge for my dad and I'll feel better now.' She looked up at me, 'I will – won't I?'

'Of course you will,' hardly a whisper came out as my lips formed the words. I was desperately trying to think.

We stood for a long time, our eyes closed, holding each other. I couldn't speak because of the tumult inside my head.

She tightened her arms around me, 'I was so angry, Piet. I've been angry ever since it happened. I could not let this soldier live. My dad was not even a soldier. They shot him without reason. I killed this German not only for myself, even more for my mum. I hear her crying at night. She can't cope. They should have shot her as well, she says. What is she going to do? Tell me that.'

'I know, I know.'

If my dad or mum had been killed I would want to do

the same thing. She had every right to kill this German, except – the war was over. He was no longer the German soldier. Now he was only a boy dressed in my clothes. I shook my head again, hoping to clear it.

Kurt was dead. It had happened because of the war. Anja was still at war. Maybe for her and for a lot of others it would never be over. I understood why she had killed the German even if it was wrong.

The fog of confusion began to lift from my brain. Whatever we decided to do, no one, least of all Mum or Dad, must know about it. Dad would immediately call the police and Anja would be arrested and sent to prison.

'I understand, Anja. I don't blame you. Now let's think what we can do about him.' I was stroking her hair. 'Everyone is at the street parties and that's a good thing. No one will care about a dead German. Today most people would cheer you.'

'I don't want that,' she said softly. 'Could we put him in the alley and pretend we know nothing about him?'

'No, the police will find us with their questions, trying to trip up whoever they suspect. They'll probably try it on everyone in the street and Kurt was in our house. My dad will happily volunteer that information.'

It became clear to me what had to be done. 'There's one thing we can do. We'll bury him. Tonight, when it's dark.'

'But where?'

'Right here in this garden. De Groot next door is the only one who'd be able to see us from his house. Of course he won't be home. He'll be out celebrating like everyone else. It'll be quiet here tonight and if we bury him deep enough he'll never be found.'

Anja brushed away her tears and looked into my eyes. She was calmer now. 'I knew you would know what to do. You will help me, Piet. You must always be there for me.'

'I will be, my love.' I meant this more than anything I had ever said.

I took the biscuits off my handkerchief and wrapped the knife in it. I took her hand. Not looking down at Kurt again, we left the cellar. We didn't meet anyone in the alley and we heard people shouting and celebrating in the street as if everything was wonderful.

Back at her house she took the knife from me and calmly washed the blood off it under the outside tap. I felt cold. The water turned the tiny specks of dried blood on her arm from almost black to pink. It flowed down to her hand and between her long, slim fingers in thin streaks. She let the water run until it ran clear. The red swirled into the drain and then it was as if the blood had never been there.

She shook the drops of water off the knife and went into the kitchen to put it back into her father's fishing bag.

We must get rid of that knife, I thought. I will cut up the blade with a hacksaw or break it and throw the pieces into a canal, not all in the same place, and a long way from home. The German's uniform in the shed? I must burn that.

I washed my hands and rinsed my hankie. I knelt down and held my head under the tap. I let the cold water run on my neck for some seconds and turned my face from side to side to feel its numbing effect on my temples.

'Come, I'll get you a towel,' Anja said.

We were back in her room. How did I get there? She had partly opened the curtains and stood naked before me. I saw her long slim body with its small high breasts but even the down-covered triangle could not focus my thoughts. In the instant her father's knife plunged into Kurt's chest, my life had been split into two. Everything that had happened to me before that moment was now insignificant, of no consequence. That part of my life was young and carefree. Everything that would happen from now on, everything I would experience or do, would for the rest of my life be coloured by the soldier's death. Would I ever be able to banish his wide open, beseeching eyes from my head any more than I would stop hearing that last *'Hilfe,'* that faint blood-smothered cry for help that I could not give him? He had bound Anja and me together for ever.

My body was hot and trembling as I sat on the edge of the bed. Anja began to take off my clothes, slowly this time. Her eyes were on my face. I didn't want to look at her. I wanted to stop her, yell at her, "We can't do this, not now. How can we when that boy is lying there dead?" Yet, I didn't stop her cool hands. When I turned to her it was as if I were in a dream and saw everything through Kurt's eyes.

She began to kiss me, first my lips, then gently, my eyes, my cheeks, my neck, my shoulders, my chest. I felt nothing. I didn't want to feel anything. Anja went on kissing me until slowly, against my will, my body responded. The trembling lessened, then stopped. Her kisses began to sting like hot coals, up, down, lingering here, then there, then moving up again, my breathing quickened. She kissed the inside of my thigh and Kurt's eyes were gone. I fell back onto the bed and pulled her on top of me.

CHAPTER SEVEN

The noise of the street parties belonged to a different life, a life that I would never again be part of, a life where pleasures were simple, like coming home hungry and asking Mum what was for dinner or having a cold and being allowed to miss school.

Anja and I had lain in each other's arms for some time, not talking much, just being.

At last I stirred. 'We'd better go and join in. We'll be missed.'

The party was concentrated on the square where four streets met. A great mass of people had gathered, all of them intent on making as much noise as possible. Old men and women with red faces were furiously blowing on whistles. Kids, some with metal drums or large wooden rattles, added to the din.

A band was playing full blast on the pavement. Anja and I danced as best as we could, copying the older people. It felt delicious holding her like this and to feel her body against mine. I wanted her again. Anja's bright eyes made me almost forget what had happened. I was in love and I was her man and I was holding my woman and she was holding me. I knew she loved me and I no longer cared about the dead German. We would take care of him later and everything would be beautiful again.

When it began to get dark, I raised my eyebrows at Anja. 'Now?'

She nodded and we made our way through the dancing crowd, holding hands. Dad caught my eye and winked. I smiled back at him and felt disappointment. It would have been so good if I had been able to tell Dad what had happened and believe that he would help us, take care of it for us. I knew that wouldn't happen. It was up to Anja and me.

Once off the street, we made our way through the back alleys, collected a spade from our shed and minutes later were at the back of the bombed-out house. I'd already decided to dig between two bushes, as tall as myself. One was the raspberry bush that I had raided year after year for its fruit. I didn't know the name of the other one. We were out of sight there; it felt safe.

Anja crouched behind the remnants of the fence and watched in case someone strayed along the alley, lovers perhaps, looking for a quiet spot.

The earth was soft, very sandy, and even though digging into it was easy, I quickly became tired and worked more and more slowly, my clothes soaked with perspiration. I stopped when I'd dug about three quarters of a metre down.

'I think that's big enough.'

Anja looked down at the hole. 'It looks as if you'd fit in, so he will too.'

'Let's get him.'

We entered the cellar. The blood on his chin had dried black. The cellar had always smelled of damp earth. Now it was different, more like stale sweat and urine.

I had imagined and hoped that he might have got up and disappeared, that it had all been a terrible dream. By what was left of daylight we saw that he was still very much there and still very dead. I looked away from his staring eyes. I thought I ought to close them.

'I'll take his feet.' Anja was calm and efficient.

His body was stiff and we carried him like a plank of wood, not a very heavy one. As we crossed the garden, the moon came out showing his washed-out blue skin and his eyes large and glittering. Why hadn't I closed them? I felt like dropping him and running away.

'He looks awful.'

'He'll never hurt anyone again,' Anja answered.

We put him down next to the hole. I didn't want to look at him even though I said, shivering, 'I must close those eyes.'

I squatted down and tried not to look directly at him as my hand moved his eyelids. The skin was cold. It no longer felt like human skin yet he still looked like a person. I got up. One of his legs was bent, the knee sticking up and, overcoming my repulsion, I pushed it with my foot. It was locked and refused to stay down.

'Come on.' I was sweating and tried again. 'God!' I jumped on his thigh. There was a thud and it stayed flat.

The hole was only about forty centimetres wide. We dropped him in and he fitted neatly. We looked down at him. In the half-light I could make out the dark stain of blood on my old shirt.

I saw Anja's hands shake. She turned away and I

began to shovel the soil on top of him, not looking down. Ten minutes later we trampled the soft earth down. We were standing on his face. Though it was the face of the enemy, what made it horrible was the fact that he had been breathing and talking to me only a few hours earlier.

'The earth looks too fresh.'

'Of course,' I said. 'We'll build it up a bit higher and put some rubble on it.'

I found some bricks, thinking that they would compact the earth and before long nothing would show that the ground had been disturbed.

We ran off back to our house and put the spade back into the shed. Anja followed me into the shed and closed the door behind her. The light of the three-quarter moon threw an oblong of silver through the window onto the wooden floor. She took my hand and pulled me towards her. She was leaning against the rough timber wall and had closed her eyes, her lips parted. I kissed her, taking my time. Without speaking, she pulled up her dress and at once I went into her, slowly, kissing her face, her neck, her hair. I rode up into her body and Kurt's deathly face faded away. Anja let out a cry and I laughed and moaned at the same time. We stood still, breathing hard, the sound of the street party far away.

I was certain that we had thought of everything, and no one would ever find Kurt's body, or maybe in fifty years' time, and by then who would care?

'Thank you, Piet,' Anja whispered.

'We're together, no need to thank me.'

'You're my brave man. You could have panicked and run away screaming that I had killed the German.'

Johannes Kerkhoven

'No. I could never have done that. I'm happy about what we did. It was right. He was the enemy.'

She held my head between her hands. 'I'm so lucky,' she whispered.

At last I moved. 'Let's go back and celebrate.'

I felt proud to have done this for Anja. It was a rounding off of the war. A German had paid for killing Anja's father and I had protected her from being punished for it.

'Will you tell your mother?'

Anja shrugged then shook her head. 'No. If she did know would it help her?'

'No, she would worry about the Nazi being buried so close to her house. We can't tell a single soul.'

'You're right. It has to be our secret for ever.' I held her against me. 'I love you and I see keeping this secret as the symbol of our love.'

Outside the shed, the soft moonlight was bright and we made our way towards the party. Walking onto the square we were in time to see a neighbour take his turn on the slide. Hand in hand Anja and I stopped to watch.

The all-wooden construction looked like a medieval children's slide. At the top, where the man now stood, was a cart ready to race down along rails. He got into the cart, and was handed a wooden lance. 'He has to put the lance through that ring,' I said.

Another man placed a bucket of water on a ledge.

'I see,' Anja pointed. 'If he doesn't put the lance through the ring, he'll get that bucket of water over him.'

We watched as the cart hurtled down. The roar of the crowd was deafening as the man missed putting the lance through the ring and was drenched.

State of Guilt

Dad was already waiting for his turn at the top of the slide. I waved at him. He spotted me and waved back. The way he held the pole he looked like a knight at a joust.

Dad pushed off, holding the lance rock-steady, he put it straight through the ring. A great moan of disappointment went up.

'Trust Dad,' I said.

CHAPTER EIGHT

'I wonder if that German soldier we had in the house will ever get back to Germany,' Dad said the next day.

My breath stopped at the unexpected mention of Kurt but I managed to laugh with him despite my burning cheeks. Germans were no longer part of our new life, not today, not ever. We didn't have to worry about Kurt coming back.

Mum always knew when I was lying or had done something I should not have. I expected her to see at once that my laughter was not real. The exhilaration we all felt because of the liberation was still too fresh in her mind for her to sense my guilt and my panic subsided.

Now that I had time to think about the killing, I wanted to cry because I hadn't been able to stop Anja. Although I had closed his accusing eyes before we buried him, I kept seeing them open and the shovels of earth falling and Anja and me trampling the earth on to them. He had come to me for help and I had failed him and Anja and myself.

I felt old. I'd experienced war, I had buried a German

and I had a lover. I had seen people dead by the side of the road with most of us walking past, glad it wasn't us who had died from hunger or being shot or bombed.

All of our family had survived. You could have died walking down the street. I burnt my fingers once when I picked up a hot fragment of a bomb, that fell out of the sky missing me by about two feet. The Germans had thrown loads of ammunition away when they were retreating. A boy I knew found a live forty millimetre shell. He put it in a vice, hit it with a hammer and blew off his hand. A school friend in the next street caught diphtheria and died. One day he was there. The next he was gone. He had bright red hair.

Albert caught the disease as well, but recovered. When we took him home from the hospital he was too weak to walk more than a few steps. There were no cars so we walked Albert home sitting on a bicycle, Dad holding the handlebars.

* * *

Not having to go to school had been good. It was difficult to get used to the discipline of the classroom again. As the schools re-opened we were expected to be there all day long. I was restless. I wanted to do well but only to get it over with so I could get a job. If I could manage that, Mum and Dad might consider me grown up and I would be able to live my own life together with Anja. That's what I wanted most of all. Once I was sixteen and could earn money they wouldn't be able to stop me.

* * *

One magical afternoon of mild weather Anja and I cycled to the woods.

'Have you got them?' Anja asked.

For a moment I wondered what she meant. "Ah, you mean the chemist?'

'What else.'

'Yes, I said I would. I've got ten.'

'Did you blush?'

'No, I didn't. He looked at me for a second then handed them over without comment.'

'Good. It's good for you to do it. You are the man.'

'I don't mind at all,' I lied. While it did embarrass me to ask for condoms, I knew it had to be done. We were going to do it often, so we had to be careful or Anja would become pregnant, and that scared me. The thought of it made me sweat.

'Maybe I'll never have children,' Anja said.

'You will, later on, much later on.' I had a vision of Anja and me being married with at least three children.

We cycled along the sandy path that ran through the moor and into the woods where the young oak trees and shrubs would give us privacy.

'Look.' I pointed at a dense clump of foliage. 'There it is.'

We were out of sight lying on our thick, king-size bed of springy moss, looking up at the intense blue visible between the tops of the slim trees.

I stroked her hair. She smiled and pulled me towards her.

CHAPTER NINE

I was terrified that Kurt's body might be discovered. The rubble of the bombed out house was cleared and rebuilding began quite soon after the war. After the house was finished and Kurt was still where we had put him, I began to relax.

Rose, Anja's mother, went to work each morning. This left us alone in their house. If Mum and Dad had learned about what we did, they would have exploded with fury. They accepted that Anja and I were friends and that Anja helped me with my homework.

A year after the war ended at the Liberation Day celebrations, I asked Anja, 'Do you ever think about the German?'

She frowned and shook her head. 'Never. I only think of how much Mum and I still miss my dad.'

I felt guilty remembering. Sitting in my room, unable to concentrate on my studying, I thought how good it would be to forget all about Kurt as Anja had, never to think about him again or see his eyes in my mind as he fell dying at my feet, and hear his rasping voice,

'Hilfe …'

If I could tell someone it might help. I talked myself into thinking that I was ready to tell someone, and who else was there but my father?

One afternoon I felt particularly bad and when Dad came home from work and finally settled in his armchair, I felt ready to speak to him. I wanted to leave Anja out of it. I could say that I had found his body in the alley and at the time said nothing because I did not want to spoil our liberation day festivities.

'Dad …' I began.

I stood near his chair looking down at him, waiting for him to lower his newspaper.

'You know,' he smiled, 'they're still catching those traitors.' He waved a finger at the article he'd been reading. 'Here's a story about a member of the National Socialist Movement who didn't bother to register, as he was required to do after the war. He thought he'd get away scot-free by moving. Well, he changed his address six times after the liberation. First he went to live up North, then South, East, West, on the islands in Zeeland and who knows where else. Didn't do him any good though. Someone still recognised him, so that's another one caught, you might think.'

'Great.'

He snorted. 'I don't know why they bother searching for those traitors. It's a waste of money. They're almost always let off or even if they go to prison, it's only for a few months. Once they've done their stint they can laugh at us. They've paid for their mistakes then, haven't they?'

'I agree.' I let out a big breath. It was as if I had suddenly woken from a bad dream. The need to confess suddenly seemed pathetic. Dad's little speech had been enough of an interruption for me to stop me from behaving like an idiot. I began to feel hot when I thought of him marching me off to the police station.

I could have gone to prison for years if the police thought I had killed Kurt. What could I have said? That Anja had done it and ruin her life as well? I trembled.

I would never again give in to that insane need for confession and was annoyed at my weakness. I'd come close to disaster.

Who knows? If ever the memory of Kurt begins to dim, I might even miss him.

CHAPTER TEN

Dad decided that I didn't work hard enough at my studies, an opinion shared by the headmaster. Dad also felt that it was time for me to contribute to the family budget. So at seventeen years of age I became the assistant of Gert Kuypers, our local photographer. It coincided nicely with my wanting to earn money, my first step to independence and marrying Anja, so I did not protest. As an apprentice I started at the bottom of the ladder. My duties were mainly making deliveries and cleaning.

If Gert considered the floor dirty he would point. 'There's the broom.'

He was a practical joker who enjoyed teasing me but I didn't mind. I could see by the twinkle in his grey eyes that he liked me.

* * *

Before long Gert allowed me into the darkroom to clear away used developer and fixer and wash the trays. Soon after that I was allowed to load dark slides with film and a little later still, after exposure, develop the films.

I went to college in the evenings, where I was initiated into the history, theory and practice of photography. It's quite simple really. The silver solution darkens when exposed to light. Theory was more than that, with silver bromide crystals, positive and negative, electrical attraction.

Once I understood some of the rudiments of the technique of photographic lighting I began to move the big lamps where I felt that Gert wanted them. I was often right.

My earnings increased and although saving for my marriage to Anja was constantly on my mind, I felt that buying myself a Leica was also important. This took some time to pay off but I loved the feel of that camera and the crispness of its lens and the whisper-quietness of its shutter. I carried it with me practically all the time. Anja thought this amusing and asked me whether I loved my Leica more than I loved her.

'Don't answer that,' she said.

She meant to sound casual. Wasn't she certain of my love, or was she jealous of my love for my camera?

We didn't talk about getting married; I felt it was understood that we would.

In the last year of my apprenticeship I became Gert's deputy. He was happy to go on holiday and leave the running of the studio to me. Customers trusted me.

Most of my workload consisted of portraiture and whatever commercial work Gert threw at me. Generally it was the work he didn't feel like doing himself.

Eight months after qualifying as a photographer I was called up for National Service. They made me wear a hot, itchy, woollen army uniform. It also meant getting up at an ungodly hour, making your bed so that it did not look inviting, and going out in rain, snow or the occasional sunshine. The corporals and sergeants were determined to make men out of us.

We were instructed to march, go on parade, and learn how to kill other men efficiently. My job of taking family portraits seemed a wonderfully relaxed way of life by comparison. The worst of army life was that sometimes I would not see Anja for two weeks.

An obvious skill the army taught us is shooting at a target. It reminded me of being at a fairground. Perhaps the army thought this as well, as they supplied prizes for the best scores. I managed to regularly win a packet of cigarettes. If I aimed my rifle just a little above the centre of the target and slightly to the right, I scored a bull's-eye every time.

Then came bayonet practice. We had to run at a roughly made canvas figure filled with sand, strapped between two poles, while screaming as loudly as we could. I did it without enthusiasm and the sergeant made me do it again.

'Van Land, do you have a problem killing that enemy? Don't tickle him. If he'd been a real soldier you'd be dead!'

I growled like an angry dog, making certain that my face was turned away from him.

'Do that again. Only this time he's not filled with sand. He wants to shoot you and stick his bayonet into your belly. So go back. Scream at him. Scare him. Stab him hard and twist. Kill him!'

'Pathetic,' the sergeant said after my next attempt in his infuriatingly even voice. He unexpectedly yelled at me, 'Think. *You want to kill him.* You're getting really angry now.' He walked up to me and stood close. I could feel him spitting out the words in my face. 'Kill him. Kill him!'

I rubbed the back of my hand across my cheeks and gripped my rifle hard, pointing the bayonet at the sergeant's throat.

He stepped back, waved my rifle aside and grinned. 'That's the spirit. Now kill the enemy.'

I took a deep breath and turned towards the canvas figure. A German. I would have to think of a German. Kurt? I thought of Anja stabbing him. What if it had been Dad who had been shot by the Germans?

'Kill him!' The sergeant's voice hissed in my ear.

I looked at the sand bag man. He was Kurt and he was yelling. I screamed and ran at him. I reached him before he could get his rifle off his shoulder. I rammed my bayonet deep into his body. His rifle was pointing at me now and he fired. I felt nothing and stabbed him again and again. I heard his, *'Bitte, bitte!'* I couldn't stop. 'You killed my dad! So die, die! I stabbed him in the neck, chest and stomach, twisting the bayonet as I'd been shown. Blood squirted from his body. I kept lunging at him blindly, harder and harder, seeing him alternatively cringing and sneering at me. Then suddenly I saw Anja's face imprinted over his and I stopped.

A strong arm led me away. 'Well done, van Land. I think he's dead.'

I almost dropped the rifle in the sand. It had become very heavy. I looked at the sergeant through a mist of tears.

'That way,' his hand on my shoulder gave me something between a push and a pat. 'Next!'

'Were you pretending you stabbed the sergeant?' someone asked softly.

I nodded.

CHAPTER ELEVEN

After basic army training we were assigned to various specialist jobs. I was given the job of "Keeper of Regulations and Requisitions". After breakfast the administrative personnel were told to fall out at roll-call and go to their respective offices. Mine had two desks, a Gestetner copying machine and a huge cabinet full of forms and stationery. I was excused from most of the exercises and spent many pleasant hours talking and joking with colleagues who worked in adjoining offices, and writing long letters to Anja, which she seldom answered.

'I'm not a letter-writer, Piet,' Anja had said without embarrassment.

I was selected for guard-duty over the Christmas period. Apart from not being able to see Anja, which was awful, it was not all negative, I thought. At home Mum and Dad would badger me to go to church and sing carols. As a special favour Dad might have given me a small glass of red wine. Grocer's wine, he called it.

To celebrate, every soldier had brought a bottle of whatever he fancied. My choice was lemon-flavoured jenever. Though not as strong as the pure jenever, the alcohol content of twenty odd per cent still posed a considerable challenge.

Off-duty we were comfortable in our warm wooden barracks, safe from the freezing cold. Whirling, fine powdery snow had deposited a thin white carpet of snow on the tarmac outside, while most of it had collected wind-driven against the barrack walls to a height of a good metre.

At around seven on Christmas Eve a huge corporal accompanied by two privates came into our barrack, calling out my name.

'You've found me,' I said and assumed I had infringed some regulation.

'You're Keeper of Requisitions, aren't you, van Land?'

'I am that man, I confess. I'll come quietly.'

'Good. We need a Requisition Form to take a jeep out of camp.' His hands were in his pockets.

'Where's the order?' I was suspicious as orders were always signed by an officer. He knew that as well as I did.

'Well, I haven't got one. Still, it's Christmas and we want to get out of the camp for a bit. If we weren't so far from town we'd walk – but look at the weather,' he grinned. 'You needn't worry. We'll be back in a couple of hours.'

I wondered what my position would be if they had an accident on the icy roads. On the other hand, what the hell. You can't afford to be unpopular in the army.

'Well, you won't get me into trouble?'

The corporal laughed. 'You can trust me. I personally guarantee it.'

I knew that I was probably being stupid. Nevertheless I said, 'Okay, wait here. Help yourself to a drink.'

'You're a great guy, van Land.'

"God," I thought, shaking my head, "what am I doing." I was not too drunk to think ahead and anticipate the worst. All the books and forms were numbered and records had to be kept showing where each went. I took the precaution of tearing the form out of a new book of orders, the last one of my numbered stock and hid this book behind the great metal cabinet that held all my stationery supplies.

As soon as the corporal had the bit of paper in his great paw, he turned to his friends. 'Come on, guys, we're gonna have some fun,' he yelled and, slamming the door, they left the barracks.

We drank a few more jenevers and then some more.

Jaap, a farmer from Zeeland, had drunk faster and more than anyone. He was a big blond chap with huge fists, always good natured and his pink face was generally placid. He had a slow broad smile and at regular intervals would produce his bright red handkerchief and noisily blow his nose into the farmer-sized sheet of cotton.

That Christmas his tolerance for alcohol didn't stretch to keeping him upright. We helped him to his bed. At once Jaap began to snore. After a few minutes we thought we might wake him, then he stopped snoring and began to talk in his sleep. He was obviously addressing a girl. We gathered around his bed. Van Nes began to answer Jaap as if he were the girl.

'Come and sit next to me.'

'Will you behave yourself?' Van Nes answered in a high voice.

Jaap was moaning. 'Oh, come on. I really love you, you know I do and I need you right now.'

'Oh, I want you too, Jaap. Stop it. Let me take off my knickers first, you impatient brute,' Van Nes said.

At that moment some fool laughed rather loudly and Jaap blinked and sat up. He shook his head and rubbed his eyes. He saw us all standing by his bed and realised what had been happening.

'You bastards.'

His face took on the colour of his red handkerchief. He looked from one grinning face to the other making up his mind who to hit.

Tom brought over a bottle of jenever and put it in Jaap's big fist. 'Here, Jaap, this is what you need.'

Jaap took the bottle.

We all smiled at him. 'Go on Jaap, take a swig.'

We watched his face lose its tension. His eyebrows settled and he managed a smile. He took a long gulp and passed the stone bottle back. 'You could at least have let me sleep until I put it in, you arseholes.'

He was awake again, and joined us at the table where we told filthy jokes and continued drinking.

Before the end of the night I'd drunk and laughed so much that I had forgotten all about being miserable, all about the corporal and his jeep, and everything else including Anja and Kurt. At one point I passed out.

CHAPTER TWELVE

Christmas over, I travelled home and was devastated to find that Anja had gone to stay with her aunt. I spent a boring New Year's break at home. Rose, Anja's mother, apologised on her behalf. Anja had written a letter, which she had forgotten to post. She'd recently started a new job and had been busy.

Things had changed between Anja and me. She was distant. I felt that I could no longer reach her. I felt panic at the thought that she might want to end our relationship. Had we become too used to each other? Had I taken her love for granted? Was it possible that my Anja was seeing someone else? It would be at least two unending and unbearable weeks before I could expect to be home again.

On the morning I was to return to camp, I took a walk past Kurt's grave. The bushes on either side of his grave had grown and their snow-covered branches were almost touching. I shivered as I remembered how we'd buried him. He still provided that link between Anja and me.

'Happy new year!' the new owner of the rebuilt house called out to me as he came out of his back door, carrying his coal scuttle.

'Happy new year to you too.' I quickly walked on.

Back at camp, I felt unhappy and frustrated. During the first week I wrote three light-hearted letters to Anja, pretending that everything was normal between us. In reply there was one short note. I wanted to go home and speak to her, tell her how much I'd missed her.

There was a backlog of various forms and orders to print on my Gestetner. I was busy and glad about that; it provided some distraction. My thoughts spiralled endlessly around Anja.

One of the orders that needed printing set out the programme of a night exercise on the nearby moor. We were going to be instructed in night-fighting – in the snow. The exercise was scheduled to start at zero hundred hours. As expected, I received requests for forms, lots of forms.

Here was my chance to see Anja. I threw out some of the ones I knew would be needed for the night exercise, so I would have to make a train journey to The Hague, where the Central Stationery Office was located, to get new supplies. It meant a day away from the camp for two of us, as I always asked for and was granted another private to help me carry the boxes of forms. One of us could then have the day off. In the afternoon we'd meet up again to go back to camp together.

I managed to telephone Anja at work and she agreed to meet me for lunch. At once I felt better. Van Nes was happy to go to the stationery office by himself.

Our camp was away from the township. As the

warrant-officer was walking outside our barracks, I asked him, after saluting, if he could get someone to drive us to the station. Warrant-officer van Nieuweslink was a conscript as I was. He was a small man by army standards with narrow shoulders and grey eyes like shirt buttons. There was a perpetual frown between them and we called him Pip-squeak.

'Why do you want a lift to the station, van Land? It's only three kilometres. Leave earlier and walk.'

'That's stupid. I always get driven to the station,' I said. 'It's at least an hour's walk.'

'Are you telling me I'm stupid, van Land?'

'No. Would I? But I think the fact that we're not getting a car when we are on army duty seems unreasonable.'

He had the habit of talking out of the side of his mouth, and one of his teeth, half gold, glistened. I felt like laughing at him and did so, out loud. It felt wonderful. I didn't think about what could happen next. Whatever it might be, the feeling of release was worth it. I was no longer being bullied. I was controlling him, not the other way around and I was going to see Anja.

'Stand to attention,' he said. 'You're going to be put on report for this.'

After glancing in all directions, I saw there was no one around. 'So what. Put me on report then. I'll just deny it.' I laughed again, and walked away.

'You'll be on report,' he called after me.

What can they do to me, I thought. They can't very well shoot me. The war is over, so why act as if it isn't.

We managed to hitch a ride with a friendly sergeant and I forgot about the warrant-officer..

* * *

Johannes Kerkhoven

Anja and I had time for a coffee and a sandwich. She wore a white blouse I had not seen before and a new straight, navy skirt. She had also been to the hairdressers. Her hair had been cut fashionably short. I felt a pang that the thick blond tresses I loved so much were lost. However, her eyebrows were drawn together, more than usual. She sat on the edge of her chair, elbows against her body and she held her back very straight. Not a hint of the slight tilt of the head and her eyes hardly met mine. She looked down at her food or past me into the distance.

'Anja, is something wrong?'

She shook her head. 'I've got to get back to work, Piet. We're very busy. If I'm late I'll lose my job.'

'Of course.' I knew her well enough not to question her. Seeing her without having the opportunity to talk for any length of time left me more miserable than I'd been before.

* * *

The next day I was summoned to the captain's office. That reminded me of the warrant-officer's threat. The captain was a professional soldier with short light grey hair and a moustache and eyebrows that were still black. He always spoke to us in a fatherly manner.

I marched in, saluted and gave my name and serial number. He took his time shuffling papers.

'This is a very serious matter, van Land.'

'Yes Sir, thank you, Sir.'

'The charge is that you have failed to obey the command of an officer. If this had been war time you would have been shot. Do you have anything to say?'

'Yes Sir, no Sir, that's correct Sir. Thank you, Sir.' I

thought, if we'd been in battle I would've shot the squeaky little bastard first.

He looked at the charge sheet and then at me. 'Why did you disobey that command?'

'I needed a car and was told to walk from the camp to the station on army business.'

'Is that unreasonable?'

'I thought – no Sir.'

Although I had planned my defence, I changed my mind. I was bored with the daily routine of getting up early, lining up on the parade ground and running off stencils. I wondered what he'd do.

The captain didn't say anything for some moments. He looked at the papers, at me, then at the papers again. Trying to make up his mind? Probably didn't like Pipsqueak either.

'You leave me no choice,' he said. 'Disobeying orders is very serious.'

You've already said that, I thought.

'I am going to sentence you to eight days solitary confinement.'

Looking at the blank wall behind him, I decided if I looked shocked or laughed it would be going too far. A month in a cell would be boring. Eight days would be a break from daily routine. There would be time to think about Anja.

'Yes Sir, thank you, Sir.'

'Van Land.'

'Yes Sir?'

'Stop saying thank you Sir.'

I suppressed a smirk. 'Yes Sir, thank you, Sir,' I said and gave him a smart salute.

He closed his eyes. 'Dismissed.'

Still saluting, I turned on my heels, clicked them and marched out of his office.

CHAPTER THIRTEEN

I presented myself at the detention block at ten on a Thursday morning. A sergeant told me to stand to attention. After giving my name and serial number I was allowed to stand at ease.

He had to fill in a form that was large enough to hold my entire history and leave room for both my parents' and grandparents' particulars as well. By the time he'd done that, it was after ten-thirty.

The sergeant told me to hand over my belt and shoelaces, and at last took me to my cell. It was quite clean, two and a half paces wide, three and a half paces long. The walls were made of cement and the floor was concrete. Apart from a wooden bunk, it was totally bare. No toilet, not even a bucket to piss in.

There was a three inch thick metal door with a peep hole and opposite, in the outside wall, high up near the ceiling, was the barred window; about a foot in height and going along the width of the cell.

I soon learned, with some disappointment, that solitary confinement in the army was not what I'd expected it to be. I was not going to get any raw experience. It wasn't like a real prison. Every morning they woke you at seven-thirty and let you out of the cell for a shit, a wash, a shave and breakfast. At eleven they gave you half an hour of fresh air. For lunch and dinner you were out of your cell again. The whole day was broken up into chunks of time and went quickly. You were even allowed books and writing material.

Moek and Dad got a letter. I asked them if it rained at home and took a whole paragraph to tell them that it didn't rain in the camp. I neglected to tell them about the solitary. They'd only advice me to be a good boy and follow orders. My letters to Anja was rather longer.

> Dearest Anja,
> God, I miss you. Being in this cell makes the pain of being away from you ten thousand times more intense. I have so much time to think about you and that's also wonderful, because I would rather think about you than about anyone or anything else and without any distractions. I think about your hair, your face, your wonderful body. If I were a composer, I would write you a "Meditation to the Body of Anja". I could think about all of you for ever. And will.
>
> You stop me noticing the bare walls, the damp air and you even make me ignore the bit of sky that I can see through the barred window. I've dreamed about you more than once. Last night you had your legs wrapped tightly around my body. It was wonderful, except that when I woke you

weren't there. I'd been turning in my sleep and the bloody blanket had wrapped itself around me. I'm so looking forward to seeing you the weekend after next. You will be there, won't you?

As I mentioned in my last letter, I'm in and out of my cell all day long. There's even entertainment in here. The thick metal door to my cell opens to the outside. It's easy to slam shut and does so with a loud, echoing bang, but it's hell to open as it sticks rather badly. When the soldier on prison-guard duty needs to open it to let me out for breakfast or whatever, he bangs on the door and kicks at it while calling out to me to push.

A couple of times in the morning, I pretended to be asleep and let him curse for a while. When he finally managed to open it, I peeked out from under the blanket and said in my sleepiest voice, 'Aaaah. Good morning.'

I'm going to be let out to go to church tomorrow. When we come back from there we'll have our Sunday lunch. The food is bearable during the week, while on Sundays it's better. I heard that we'll be having soup first, then roast beef with potatoes and green beans, followed by pudding.

We're allowed cultural books. This afternoon I finished a great book about Goya, the Spanish painter. Of the illustrations in it I particularly liked the drawings. Then I've still got a novel to read. It's thick. *Ted Pentecost* by Howard Spring, probably sloppy. Still it will pass the time.

When we're let out for air in the morning, we're herded into a courtyard that is enclosed on three sides by the building. The fourth side is a high wire fence that separates us from the rest of the camp. Almost every time I'm out there a few of my friends come over to have a chat and bring me something. Usually chocolate or cigarettes. After they have been there for a few minutes the sergeant invites them to join me inside, or clear off.'

So you see, my darling woman, I am surviving.
I send you lots of kisses or, if you prefer, one continuous one. Dying to hold you,
>   love,
>   Piet

After I had finished the letter I felt drained and started to think about Kurt again. What if his body were found? Will I finish up in a cell like this?

The thought of it made the air in the cell feel heavy, damp and cold. I rubbed my arms and looked up. I hadn't noticed before how low the sloping ceiling was. I could almost touch it as I could touch both walls when I stretched out my arms. Those cold, white-washed walls were closing in on me. I badly wanted space and air. I felt the urge to scream and kick at the impregnable door. I sat down on the wooden bunk for some minutes, sweating and trembling. I began to breathe deeply, a very long breath in, count to five while holding it, then expelling as much of the used-up air as I could. I calmed down. I'm safe and the bushes are covering his grave. He looks like a mummy by now with the roots of the bushes winding themselves around him tighter and tighter.

CHAPTER FOURTEEN

I had leave the following Friday and Anja surprised me. I had expected her to be cool and distant towards me, but she was waiting for me and she was her old loving self. She had the key to a friend's flat. I told Mum and Dad that I had to go back to camp the next morning, so Anja and I spent the weekend together.

She put her arms around me. 'My God, I've missed you, Piet.'

'Me too,' I said, 'so much.'

'Ah,' she held me at arm's length. 'You look fit. I think you're enjoying army life. You even make being locked up sound like fun, while I'm working in the shop serving fussy housewives. I feel like screaming sometimes. They try on every pair of shoes in the shop and then walk out without buying anything. Take me with you to the army. Smuggle me into your barracks. I promise I won't be in the way.' She stood back.

I laughed, 'What a great idea. It would make my life perfect, though I'm not sure you would like the food. Now show me that bedroom again.'

'Only if you promise to behave when you get back tomorrow. The sooner you get out of the army the better. You mustn't get into any more trouble. I want you here, not in an army cell.'

'My darling, I swear it,' and kissed her nose, her forehead, her lips.

During that weekend we only left the flat to visit a small restaurant around the corner to eat our evening meal. On Sunday night as I took the train back to camp I was totally convinced that Anja loved me as much as she had always done and always would.

* * *

Eighteen months in the army is an eternity yet demob-time inevitably comes around. At long last we found ourselves on the train to Utrecht. Our mood was exuberant and we were all full of plans for civilian life. As soon as I was working again I would ask Anja to become my wife.

Some way into the journey home, I was staring out of the window thinking about my future happiness, not seeing the pine forests speeding by. I contemplated going back to my job with Gert. It didn't seem very attractive. It would be like going backwards although I would go and see him. I'd already decided to move out of Mum and Dad's house. I needed my freedom, my own place where Anja could come and stay with me as often as she wanted to.

CHAPTER FIFTEEN

The garden where we'd buried Kurt had been neat and tidy for some years. The house had been rebuilt to match the older ones next to it.

Kurt's dead eyes haunted me occasionally in a dream or nightmare although it became easier to push the memory of him aside each time after I'd seen his grave undisturbed.

Even if I could forget about the soldier for a while, I wasn't like Anja. She seemed to have the ability to put everything about that day out of her mind which seemed callous but I understood. Killing the German soldier had been her way to exorcise the memory of seeing her father lying on the pavement in a pool of blood.

Anja had started a job in Amsterdam and I'd decided to accept a position with the studio of Richard Oosterdaal in Utrecht. As a consequence we saw less of each other. I wasn't happy about it and after not seeing her for a month, I phoned her and said that I would like to spend some time with her. She seemed reluctant at first, but as I insisted she agreed to meet the following weekend. I expected that we would spend all of Saturday and Sunday together.

It was good to see her but when we kissed she kept her lips firmly closed and she made certain that our bodies hardly touched.

She asked me several questions about my photography and then began to relate a minor drama that had taken place at work.

Her eyes hardly met mine. 'What is it, Anja, is something wrong, work perhaps?'

'No, no. Work is fine.'

'Well what then, is it us?'

'Yes, Piet. We haven't met for weeks, have we?'

'That's the way it is while you're working in Amsterdam and I am in Utrecht.'

'It's not enough.'

She looked at me, her face taut.

'I see, what are you telling me Anja?'

'We're growing apart, Piet. I am changing and I am no longer what you need in a woman and you are no longer the Piet of four years ago.'

'I am and I love you just as much now as I did then. More even. Yes, Anja, my love has grown more mature. After our last weekend together I felt …'

'Yes Piet, I wanted to talk to you about that. I'll never forget those two nights we spent together. I wanted to be with you so very much, and the lovemaking was all I could have wished for. Yet that weekend helped me to make up my mind. Afterwards I felt elated for a short time. Then when I was back in Amsterdam I felt – well, empty. There is not enough fire in our relationship, not any more and I knew then that it is restricting for both of us.

State of Guilt

I stared at her, unable to speak. When I found my voice, I couldn't prevent it from trembling. 'What do you mean? I … You and I … the ring I gave you.'

She was not wearing it, and it appeared in her hand. She looked straight at me her eyes without expression. She put the ring on the table in front of me, in the middle of the wet patch my glass had made.

I looked at it and then back at Anja. 'What are you doing?'

'I'm giving you back your freedom.'

'I don't want that.' I watched her face for some moments, 'Have you met someone?'

'Do you remember Maarten?'

I'd met him once. 'Yes, of course, I do. The schoolmaster.'

'Well, I've been seeing quite a lot of him lately.'

'What do you mean, seeing a lot of him?'

'I – well, I've become fond of him, quite fond. He asked me to marry him some time ago. Of course I said no. Then he asked me again. I made him wait.'

'He asked you even though you are engaged to me?'

'Engagement is not marriage; it's a time to think and I did think, Piet. I love you. You know that. I love you as my closest friend. Now I've come to the conclusion that marriage to you would not be right. It would not work. I am not the woman for you. I would make you unhappy.'

'How can you say that? I always thought … God, I don't know what's happening to you.'

She touched my hand. I withdrew it.

'I don't want you to feel hurt, Piet.

'God. What would you do if you did?'

'I thought you'd understand. I thought you might have become interested in someone else as well. And why not? We don't see much of each other.'

'So the weekend we spent together last month didn't mean anything?'

'I already said, Piet. I shall always treasure the memory of that and all the other times we've had together. Now it's time to move on, to live the lives we are meant to live. Too much happened in our shared past. You have never really let go of that. I may as well say it. You feel guilty and worry about that dead German. Be honest with me, Piet.'

'I hardly ever think about him now.'

'Hardly ever. You've said it. It would not work, Piet. You'll find someone much more suitable for you than I can ever be.'

I sat staring at her, not believing what I was hearing. Then I knew. 'You have already made up your mind, haven't you?'

Her hand reached out to her glass. She stopped and was hardly audible. 'Yes, I am going to marry him.'

'You can't, you can't. Won't you at least think about it? It would be wrong. You and I belong together.'

'Come on.' She shook her head and took my hand again, firmly, and her clear eyes held mine with an icy determination. 'Don't think it's been easy for me, Piet. I have thought about this for a long time. You can believe that. It is best for both of us. I am certain of that and if you love me you will want what is best for me. So wish me happiness. I do want you to approve, Piet. He's such a good man.

'Yes I wish you happiness but with me. How could I

approve? How can you ask for my blessing when you're destroying me.'

'You will thank me one day, Piet. I know.'

I could see that she meant everything she had said. A flood of words whirled around in my head. She sat there calmly, as if she had told me she had just returned a new dress. I could not bear to look at her. I wanted to run and got up, paid the waiter at the till and without another word walked away. I felt my life had ended.

She followed me out. 'Piet,' she called, 'let's not part like this.'

I broke into a run. I couldn't bear to let her see my tears.

I sat in a café hearing her words again. I had been so sure of her. I could not accept this sudden rebuttal. Had she already decided to marry Maarten while she was making love to me?

He was taking my place. I hated him. I felt the kind of pain I had felt before. It was my earliest memory. I was three years old and Albert had been born a week or two earlier. Mum let me watch him at her beautiful, warm breast. He was sucking eagerly with the smug look of pure happiness on his face. What was he doing there? I should be there. She's *my* mum. From that day on I could no longer climb on her knee and I hardly ever felt Mum's arms around me. "He" was always there.

'Go and play now, Piet,' she would say, or, 'Not now, Piet, Mum's tired.'

Even when I did have the luck to be in her arms, Albert would start to cry and she'd put me down. He was always the nuisance, ever the spoilsport. Why did he have to be born? He had ruined everything for me, and now

Anja had done the same, when I thought she and I would be together for ever.

Shortly before her marriage Anja wrote to me. I imagined her sitting at her table writing and saw her hand slide across the paper. That small slim hand that I had so often felt on my trembling body. The faint smell of perfume that her wrist had left on the paper made me bring it to my nose and breathe in deeply.

> Dearest Piet
> I was too blunt when I told you about my marriage to Maarten but I thought you would have guessed that my feelings for you had changed. Dear Piet, I did not mean to hurt you, and you know I will always love you. We are very special to each other. We always will be. You know that too. I did not mean for things to happen this way and I am sorry. I want you to know that I will always be grateful for having you in my life, and I am determined always to keep you there. We know each other better than anyone else can ever know us and maybe that is why we will not be together. At the same time knowing each other the way we do is also the most wonderful thing in my life. That will never change. Remember how I used to call you my Teddy bear? Piet, I have already decided that my first son will be called Ted. So you see, I will think of you for ever.
> Yours always,
> Anja

My first impulse was to burn the letter. How could

State of Guilt

she write this letter? I was being dismissed. I heard her message loud and clear: Thank you for loving me. Now I don't love you any more. It was an insult to my love for her. I gave her my all, I was even happy to commit a crime for her. I would die for her and now she waltzes off to a new life not giving me another thought.

* * *

Richard gave me a large box of books to photograph, most of them with mirror-like glossy covers that were devils to light without unwanted reflections. I was grateful for the challenge and the urgency of the job. It distracted me yet Anja was still so powerfully on my mind that I had to stop several times and fight my emotions. I imagined her with "him", getting a house and buying furniture together. That should be me instead of Maarten. It was wrong. I could see them getting into bed and Anja cuddling up to him as she had done to me and then … I didn't want to think any further.

Oosterdaal came into the studio and noticed I'd stopped working. 'Are you all right, Piet?'

'Yes. I …' I turned to the door and, as I walked past him, said, 'I need a shit.'

'Come into my office when you're done. I've got an urgent one for you.'

I blew my nose and got up, knowing that if I took too long, Richard would pull me off the seat. Ha, he's got an urgent one. Is the lot I'm working on no longer urgent?

His answer would be, 'This one is extra urgent.'

* * *

Anja sent me a postcard from Venice, where she and "he" had gone for their honeymoon. "The weather is not so good, but the trip on The Orient Express was wonderful and The Daniele Hotel is the best in Venice. Be happy for me?"

I threw the card onto the floor and stamped on it. Then I ripped it into a thousand pieces and flushed those down the toilet. Her letter stayed in the bottom drawer of my desk.

CHAPTER SIXTEEN

I had moved into two rooms above a shop in Hilversum. It had become impossible for me to live with my parents. They pretended to accept the fact that I no longer wanted to belong to their church when in reality they never gave up. Little hints were dropped continuously. It was embarrassing to ignore these. It seemed that they subscribed to the Chinese torture method: keep at Piet long enough and sooner or later he'll break down and fall to his knees, crying, "Please Jesus, save me".

When the job was secure and I felt that I would stay with Oosterdaal for some time, I found a flat in Utrecht, close to the studio. There was space for all my possessions and that would make the flat mine, my first home.

When I told her of my move, Mum became emotional, 'All the way to Utrecht.'

'Half an hour by bike,' I said.

I had left one suitcase with my parents when I had moved out of their home. I took it with me this time and felt that it made the break from them permanent. When I opened this suitcase in my new flat and took out the two volumes of my dictionary, some papers fell out.

'My God!' I called out as they lay in front of me on the table.

Kurt was staring at me from his identity papers. I had completely forgotten about them. It was as if his eyes jumped off the print and drilled themselves into my brain.

He gasped again, *'Hilfe ...'* And Anja and I were burying his body again. I felt fear. God! Does it all have to happen again?

He had carried the military papers, together with the photograph of himself and his chubby little sister in the top pocket of the uniform he had abandoned after he had changed into my old clothes. He had given the papers to me and asked me to send them to his family if anything should happen to him. Without thinking about any consequences I had promised.

I picked them up, amazed. The memory of those papers had been completely wiped from my mind. I had thought about Kurt, but never for one moment about his papers. That was positive. If you can forget one thing, you can forget another. As I held them in my hand, I wondered what I would do with them.

I could hear Anja laugh. 'Burn them, silly boy!'

I was not sorry for what Anja and I had done and I knew that burning the papers would be the most sensible thing to do. I also knew that I could not do that because I had made a promise to Kurt. It would be a final conscious act to send them back to Germany. I had looked after them long enough. It would be like disowning him at last, putting a full stop to the whole story. Sending him

State of Guilt

back to where he came from. He *will* be out of my life if I do that and I will never need to think or dream about him again.

I was uncertain about what motivated me. The papers made me feel uneasy–as if they were trying to control my life. If I burnt them nothing more could happen. Would posting them to Germany be a continuing of my relationship with Kurt, or finalise it? Did part of me enjoy having him in my head? Did I feel nostalgic for the war? After all there had been a positive side to that awful period. There had been solidarity and a melting away of differences between people. All of us against the common enemy. Or did I want to send those papers back to continue my bond with Anja? Could it even be a kind of daring fate to see if we would be found out? A kind of revenge on Anja that would destroy her relationship with Maarten. Would she come back to me then?

I brushed these thoughts aside. I convinced myself that I wanted to be fair, even to our previous enemies. If there were any surviving members of his family, they had a right to his papers.

It took me weeks of deliberating. My sense of correctness won out, no doubt due to my Calvinist upbringing.

Dear Family Grutz,
Maybe this letter will be returned to me in a few weeks' time, but it might just find you.
I knew Kurt Grutz during the last days of the war in Holland. He was escaping from a group of men from the resistance movement, who wanted to kill him. I thought this was wrong. I managed

to hide him for a time and I gave him some civilian clothes. That was the last I saw of him. These are his papers. He had given them to me for safekeeping.
I'm sorry I did not send them earlier. They were lost and I only recently found them again.

Yours sincerely,
Piet van Land.

As I walked to the postbox I felt a sense of finality. I dropped the papers in and walked away. Back in the flat I poured myself a jenever. To Kurt. This will put an end to him. It felt right.

CHAPTER SEVENTEEN

If anyone had told me during that winter of nineteen forty-four/forty-five, that seven years later I would be posting a letter written in that hated German language, I would have laughed. Only months after the war ended, we'd been back at school, learning our English, French and our *der, die, das* – as if there had never been a war.

I was expecting the letter that I'd sent to Germany with Kurt's papers to come back to me undelivered. When it did I would be able to forget him. I would have done my bit, done the right thing by him and by myself. We were busy at work and my social life was getting interesting. The pain of losing Anja was still there. However as time went on, I inevitably came to terms with that. My circle of friends widened. I met Gwendolyn, the daughter of a tax inspector at a friend of a friend's party. She was attractive and fun to be with. When I attempted to kiss her, she firmly forbade me to kiss her on the lips. She loved to be kissed anywhere else on her body. No place was restricted, only – never on the lips. 'I don't want germs,' she insisted. I called her "Don't-kiss-me-on-the-lips-Gwenny".

Then there was Melody. A happy name, I thought, and musical. Melody was brought up by nuns. She invited me into her bed quite soon after we met. Melody wasn't shy, yet I was not to see her naked. Even when making love, her pink slip never came off, until I wondered whether there was a surprise under it, perhaps a huge purple birthmark. I never found out.

Despite these and several other short relationships, I was hopeful that it wouldn't be long before someone would take Anja's place, that I would meet someone that I could love.

A month after I had posted Kurt's papers to München, a letter with German stamps arrived. I had no longer expected it. Damn! I had been sure that sending the papers would finally put him to rest. Why had I put my return address on the envelope? That was stupid. I'd missed the one chance of finally getting rid of him. I turned the letter over several times as if to guess its weight. I knew I would open it, and I also knew that it was going to be important. I pretended for some time that I could throw it away unopened.

> Dear Piet van Land,
> First of all, thank you very much for your letter and for Kurt's papers. Receiving those papers was a great shock to me. I could not look at them or reread your letter without wanting to cry. It brought back thoughts about that terrible time of the war and made me think about things that I had imagined I had put at the back of my mind. I am the girl in the photograph that you sent. It was taken centuries ago. I did not know that

State of Guilt

Kurt had the photograph with him and it is very precious to me, as it reminds me of the time when we were a family and we were happy. As a child I knew nothing about the horrors of war. I have spent many hours thinking about what I would write to you, but even now I can only find clumsy words that cannot convey what I feel.

I still miss my brother and sometimes have the crazy thought that he may be alive somewhere. I know this is foolish. Common sense tells me that he has died or he would have come back to us. I know I must be brave and that life must go on, although I wish it would not sometimes.

The war ended badly for everyone. So many people I knew are now dead. Except for one aunt, I am the only one of my family who is still alive. Kurt was my big brother, I always felt that he would look after me.

Many of us Germans are ashamed now that we know what we did to your country and to the world. It was all so unnecessary and it did not get Germany anything other than great misery. The whole world must be glad that we are now a broken nation with most of our fathers, husbands and brothers dead and many of our cities destroyed.

It is difficult not to think about how much Kurt may have suffered. He was only a boy, sixteen years old when he had to become a soldier. Is it possible for you to think back to that awful time when you met him and think of any more details? Could I write to the police or hospitals? As it is now, I feel I can not be at peace. I keep wondering. Is it possible that he was wounded and lost his memory? I have heard of cases like that. The worst is not knowing what has happened to him. I hope you can understand that.

If it is not too painful for you, I hope you can please write to me once more. I must try and find out what has happened to my dear brother. If it means that I will in the end discover that Kurt is never coming back, I can then try and accept that.

Yours sincerely,
Inga Grutz

I looked at the letter and read it once more. No! I told myself. I must throw it away and not think about this German again. Damn it, why did I have to put a return address, I thought again. Now I was involved. Is that what I had wanted all along? This woman did not sound like a Nazi – more like one more victim of the war. I did not want to think about Kurt being part of a family. He should remain a German soldier, an enemy, and I wanted him out of my life, instead of that he was back more strongly than ever.

For nearly a week I agonised over the letter, reading it again and again for anything I might have missed. Then I decided that I would be rational and calm and that it would only be fair to answer her letter. After all, the war was not her fault any more than it was mine and it was understandable that she wanted to know what had happened to her brother. Once she knows that he is one of many soldiers who went missing, she will accept that he will never come back.

State of Guilt

I wrote another letter. In it I told her that I had only known Kurt very casually, and had not seen him after the liberation. I was brief and when I had posted the letter I told myself that this would be the end of it.

To my relief day after day went by without a letter arriving from Germany. Kurt would be with me until I died, I knew that and I had become resigned to it. What was the saying? You can get used to anything, even being strung up. I was even getting used to being without Anja. Perhaps I would never see her again. She could live on in the back of my mind, in the same place where Kurt had set up permanent residence.

* * *

I was virtually running the photographic studio now as my boss Richard Oosterdaal, the owner of the business, spent more and more time on his collection of historical documents. So there was little time to think of possible replies from Germany.

Then, as I was about to leave for work one morning, all keyed up for a busy day, there it was on the doormat, face up with its German stamps. In this letter Inga Grutz thanked me again and would I please understand that she wanted to know more about what had happened to her brother. She'd established that he had deserted from his unit. Somewhere, someone must know what had happened to him. Could I suggest some addresses for her to write to. The police might have some records or if he was taken prisoner, would that be recorded somewhere?

I rubbed my forehead. No need to panic. It had been war time when we killed Kurt, so we did nothing wrong. Officially the German army had capitulated and what we did was certainly nowhere near as bad as what an SS unit had done in Amsterdam. When people started to run out onto the Dam, the central square, to celebrate the capitulation of the German army, SS soldiers, who had been occupying a nearby building, opened fire on them without warning and killed eight people. I couldn't imagine what it would feel like to lose someone you love very much, at the moment you think you have come through the war alive.

My next letter to Kurt's sister was even shorter than the previous one. I wanted her to know that I didn't want further contact with her. I did give her some addresses of police stations in likely locations. That would be the end of it, I felt.

Incredibly, some four months later, she wrote to me again, saying that she was satisfied now that she knew how Kurt had died. For a second my heart stopped. How could she know? As I read on, she told how the bodies of two young men had been found burnt to death in a house fire not very far from Kurt's barracks. They must have been deserters hiding in the empty house. The local fire chief remembered it very well. By a belt buckle they had found he had concluded that the two men had been Germans. Their bodies had been burnt beyond recognition. What remained of them was cremated, and the ashes buried.

> I do thank you so very much. Now I can be at peace, knowing how Kurt has died. I knew that he did not want to be a soldier. It is tragic that he died in the fire, but I feel very proud of him. Now I can think of him as a hero who was brave enough to desert his unit and thereby prove that

State of Guilt

he rejected Nazism. If he had been caught by his superiors he would have been shot without trial. You don't know how much this means to me and I shall always be grateful to you first of all for helping Kurt and then helping me to find out at last what happened to my beloved brother.

> Yours,
> Inga Grutz

This time I did not answer her letter. The story that she had accepted as the truth was plausible. It wasn't the truth, but plausibility often outperforms truth. What more could I tell her? There was no longer any reason for me to think about Kurt. At last it was all finished. It was a closed chapter now and we could all get on with our lives.

I hadn't seen or heard from Anja for a long time and I hadn't told her anything about my correspondence with Kurt's sister. I was learning to live without Anja and after all, life was good to me. There was my photography and I was meeting new people. I regularly thought I was in love but then I would ask myself: Do you need this relationship? Could you live without her?

The reason for my failure to establish a permanent relationship was clear. I could never feel for anyone what I'd felt for Anja and it seemed to me that no one ever felt for me what Anja had felt for me, even if it had ended. I never experienced the same intimacy, the trust and the friendship. Every time I met a new woman there was initial excitement, then, sometimes quickly, sometimes after a longer period, I knew that it wouldn't work.

My job was secure, though a little boring. All the

clients wanted from me was that I make them look good in their photographs.

It was in my spare time that my profession began to give me the most pleasure. I had discovered landscape photography. Ansel Adams was my hero. I wanted my photographs to equal or at least come close to the quality of his pin-sharp black and white landscapes, and dreamt of having exhibitions of my prints. My subject matter could not rival America's majestic scenery, but, thinking of our seventeenth century painters, I was happy to emulate them and never tired of our Dutch skies and our small compact cities. Many of them had not changed much over three hundred years.

Our lakes and rivers too attracted me as subjects. I was planning to go to the lakes in Loosdrecht on a particular Saturday and was anticipating the pictures I would be taking. The weather promised to be bright, so I went to bed early as I wanted to be sure that the sun would be where I wanted it to be by the time I got to the lakes. The surface of the water would, I hoped, be mirror-flat and the early morning sky clear and clean with perhaps some gilt-edged clouds thrown in.

That night, as I was waiting for sleep and the events of the day paraded themselves in front of my half-conscious mind, Kurt and his fat little sister managed to wriggle their way back into my head. I shook off the thoughts and closed my eyes, picturing myself on the lake shore, setting up the big tripod with the Hasselblad, my favourite camera for landscape photography.

CHAPTER EIGHTEEN

I was thinking of Anja's breasts as I closed the door of the garden shed, key in the lock.

'Piet!'

I wheeled around and froze. 'Kurt!' Every muscle in my body tensed. I could only stare at him.

His uniform was torn. His face was distorted into a grimace, mouth twisted, thin lips curled out, showing large canine teeth. The eyes, huge and yellow were oozing black tears. He growled, dripping long strands of pink slobber. An immense knife was embedded in his chest. He grunted with agony as he yanked it out. He raised the knife up high. The serrated edge of the blade caught a flicker of light and bright blood ran along its groove and down on to his wrist.

There was no mistaking about his intention. I began to shake violently. He sprang at me. I managed to get out of his way, but slowly, it was as if I were moving through syrup. I avoided the knife and shoved him aside. I wrestled with the shed door. It gave way and I struggled inside. As I shut the door, he pulled at it from the outside with tremendous force.

I knew I wouldn't be able to hold out against him for more than a few seconds. Sweat ran into my eyes and I desperately looked around for a weapon of some kind. My eye caught sight of the bright blue steel blade of our axe. Sharpened that morning, it was lying on the stack of pinewood I had cut earlier. The strong smell of resin was in my nostrils.

In the same instant I had let go of the door knob I felt the cold, familiar handle of the axe in my hand. It released something in me. The syrup had gone. 'I'm ready!' I screamed, my voice pitched at a ridiculously high level.

Kurt let out a hoarse cry and was inside the shed. It took only a flash for his eyes to focus in the semi-dark but it was long enough for me to use the axe with all my strength. His head split in two and one half fell onto his left shoulder, still attached at the neck by a flap of skin. He stopped, raised his hand and pushed the gory half-head back up. It was no use, it came away in his hand, strips of flesh hanging from it. With his one eye he looked at the half mask and flung it to the ground. Most of his mouth was still there, and he let out a terrifying roar.

The force of its sound wave rammed into my stomach. I wanted to be sick and stepped back as far as I could. Splinters from the rough planks of the shed wall pierced the skin of my hand.

His remaining eye doubled in size, and he slashed the air wildly with the huge knife as he came towards me.

In panic, I swung the axe. It arched through the air

and his left arm fell to the floor. A searing poker entered my chest. He's got me! He laughed triumphantly.

I was still standing and wildly brought the axe down on him again. The rest of his head rolled to my feet. His one huge eye was suddenly set in the middle of his chest and he crouched down, wary.

What was left of him swayed from side to side scanning for an opening.

He moved suddenly, knife slicing through the air so fast that I lost sight of it. I drove the axe deep into his middle. There was a sharp crack as it hit bone. As I pulled the axe away a sickly smell rose from the steaming wound. His knife had cut a large slice off my shoulder, I paid no attention to it, I was only intent on getting out.

His legs kept on running, knocking over the pile of wood, tripping over it and uselessly kicking the air. He crashed to the floor, his one arm still stabbed the air, ripped my trouser leg from thigh to ankle. My axe took off the hand holding the knife. I kicked it into the corner of the shed and was at the door. Kurt's head, whole again and much larger, began to roll towards me.

My legs were stuck to the floor. I managed to pull them free one at a time. Then I was outside and slammed the shed door ahead of the razor teeth snapping at my heels. I jammed my foot against the door and with a shaking hand turned the key. There was instantaneous hammering and thumping on the inside, and blood-curdling screeches. How long would the wooden door hold? The planks were bulging.

Crash! The blood-smeared blade of the knife cut through the thick wood as if it were smoke, and sliced into my leg.

I leapt high up into the air and took off, raced down to the end of the garden, vaulted over the fence and landed flat on my back in the hard-packed dirt of the lane.

The fall knocked the breath out of me and I was on the floor of my bedroom, shaking, my pyjamas drenched. It was five a.m. I sat up and felt my arms and legs. God!

I fell back and lay there for some minutes, staring at the ceiling, waiting for my body to quieten down. I got up and switched on the light. My camera bag and tripod stood silently near the door, waiting like old friends. They reassured me and brought me back closer to reality.

I desperately tried to swallow. I didn't want to sleep any more and went into the kitchen, drank a large glass of water and headed for the shower. As the hot water washed over my body the stark horror of the nightmare disappeared. I decided it was a trick my memory played on me – a kind of joke that my inner self thought funny. After all, Kurt had began to fade from my daily awareness, despite the fact that I had made contact with his sister. The whole episode would eventually disappear into the past.

Did the nightmare come to me, as punishment or as some kind of atonement? Surely not. Anja should be the one with nightmares.

I knew that it had been wrong to kill and bury him. It did not bother me anymore. I would bury him again with pleasure, only deeper this time. I had managed to change my memory of him to some extent. The memory of his intense staring eyes disturbed me from time to time. However, if I forced myself to recall the awful moment when I closed his eyes, they disappeared. The occasional nightmare I could live with.

I reached for my towel and switched on the radio. 'Thanks Kurt, you've given me a nice early start,' I said aloud. 'Now for my egg and bacon.'

CHAPTER NINETEEN

My fingers trembled as I opened the envelope. This wasn't meant to happen. There was to be no more contact between us. It was finished. I had told her all she needed to know. So why did she write again? She should be happy with what she'd been able to find out.

Dear Piet,

I am very grateful for all you have done for Kurt in the past. Now that I know how he died, I have not been able to leave things as they are. I want very much to come to Holland and see for myself where my dear brother died. I have also been told by your very helpful police where his ashes are buried and I feel I must visit that place. After I have done these two things, I feel I can lay him to rest and I will not bother you again.

Would you possibly do one last thing for me and arrange accommodation for me in a hotel for the two nights I plan to be in Holland, please? I would be very grateful.

                Yours,
                Inga

State of Guilt

I put the letter down and stared at it. Idiot, idiot! I stopped my fingers drumming on the edge of the table.

I did not want to see this woman, this German. I pictured her as rosy-cheeked, stocky with thick legs and her hair in a bun. She could be dangerous.

If Anja ever found out what I had done, she would be furious and say, 'Why couldn't you have left things as they were? I felt safe and happy. Is it revenge you want? Then find a way to take it out only on me. What you're doing now endangers me and Maarten, and worse my children. Is that what you want?'

I had never meant to hurt anyone. I had always wanted to do what I felt was right, and after all, in a way I had only been a bystander to the death of this woman's brother.

Some days after the letter arrived, my panic subsided and I knew I would be able to cope. Whatever had been done could not be undone and after all the German woman would only be around for two or three days and then disappear forever. Once I arrived at that conclusion I felt better and offered to be her guide during her stay in Holland. I could hardly do less.

More letters went to and fro, mainly to set a date for her visit. I put it back somewhat. I was busy and I wanted more time to get used to the idea of her coming to Holland. I suggested that she should stay in Utrecht as the train connection with Germany would be simpler from there. On the one full day she would be in Holland, we could travel to Hilversum where Kurt had been stationed during his time in the army.

When you're not looking forward to something, time tends to go quickly, and it was not long before I was standing on the platform at Centraal Station. I had been calm when I left home, then while I was waiting for Inga's train to arrive my hands felt sticky, despite the cool, late afternoon air.

My eyes scanned the rails in the distance, beyond the station. I wondered if unconsciously I had planned for events to happen the way they had. Was I fascinated with the scene of the crime? The murderer in Crime and Punishment engineered his own downfall, didn't he? Did I see myself as a criminal and did I want to be found out? It seemed a ridiculous idea.

This German woman, Inga, if she was very sensitive, might sense that there was something not quite right about me. Why would she not believe that her brother had died in the house fire? It rounded things off beautifully. It was like art. The art of manipulating life. Her mind would be put at rest. She would go back to Germany satisfied that her brother had deserted the army and, as she believed, had rejected Nazism and I would be able to forget about him.

We would meet in ten minutes time and I would act completely normally. I'd not be nervous and afraid that I might betray myself. The story that she had been told had become the truth for her and after visiting all the places where Kurt might have been she would be able to let go of the whole thing and return to Germany satisfied, marry a fat German and her brother would become a distant memory. We would never need to communicate again.

As I waited for the train to arrive, it all went through my mind again. I was unhappy that Anja had almost completely vanished from my life. After being so close – partners in love and in crime. I thought that it would have cemented our relationship to such an extent that it would last for ever. I was mistaken, Anja had betrayed me. I still felt rejection and hurt.

Anja had phoned me unexpectedly, leaving me miserable for the day. 'We're moving to Eindhoven. Maarten is starting a teaching job there.'

That meant they were going to live in a nice neat house, like a million other happy families. I did not want to know what she was doing. Despite my effort, my voice had sounded unsteady.

'Eindhoven? Will you be happy there? It's rather a boring city, isn't it?' I asked and wondered how long it would be before she would get restless.

'It's surrounded by beautiful woods, and we already have a house.'

During those first few months after we buried Kurt I experienced a closeness with Anja that I had thought could not possibly exist between two humans. She had given herself to me, all of her, her body and her soul, I had felt, and I did not care, and never would, about what I had seen her do. I considered myself privileged that she had felt free enough to do it in front of me. Whenever I remembered how Anja had pushed her father's knife into the German's chest, I also saw her body, her hard breasts and felt the swell of her belly as she pushed herself against me. I couldn't help associating the killing with the sex we had before and after it.

I would not hear from Anja for months. I never felt free to contact her. If Maarten answered the phone it might complicate her life. Then, as I began to think that I would never hear from her ever again, an envelope would arrive in the post with some trinket, like a key ring or some sweets. Never a note with it or a sender's address. My name and address were always handwritten, so that I knew immediately that it came from Anja. I never replied or sent her anything. These teasing communications would bring her back into my mind and I assumed that this was precisely what she intended. If she had not wanted to marry me or live with me, she did not want me to forget her either. Was this because of what she still felt for me or was it a kind of reminder: be strong and don't ever forget the bond that there is between us or was she amusing herself and playing with me?

Mutual friends would tell me the latest news about her. That was enough for me. She would also ring me occasionally and then, as soon as I heard her voice, I would also hear my heart beating inside my chest. After a long conversation we would invariably agree to meet for lunch at a time and place specified by Anja.

'I'll ring you soon and confirm.'

She would not ring me again for another six months or a year. We never met for lunch.

When you have not seen someone for a year, they tend to disappear from your immediate consciousness and get relegated to the box inside your head where you keep your memories. Obviously Anja was not happy with that. It was as if she was afraid that if I were to forget her, part of herself might disappear with my vanishing memory. She needn't have worried; I could never forget her or stop wanting her.

I understood the words of the song that tells of seeing your lover in a crowd of strangers. A woman in a crowd might walk in front of me, swinging her hips just as Anja did. It would bring her instantly back into my mind. If behind me someone's laugh was pitched just like Anja's, I would involuntarily turn and stare into a stranger's face.

Part of her was always with me. Sometimes it was as if she was standing right next to me. I would stand very still, not looking, afraid to lose the feeling. It could be so real that I would smell her perfume and feel my body respond. At other times I would shiver as I saw her stabbing Kurt again and coolly wash the knife under the outside tap, holding it until the water ran clear and the tiny dark spots on her bare arm that, in the running water, became thin bright red streaks and disappeared as she rubbed them vigorously, and after that being with her again in her darkened bedroom.

I was standing directly under the large platform clock and the click of the minute hand made me look up and remember where I was. Inga's train was running late.

CHAPTER TWENTY

The two unidentified German deserters who had burnt to death were a godsend of a coincidence. It had happened during the night or early morning. I remembered talking about it with Albert.

'Huh! Nothing serious about that,' he said. 'Two Germans less to worry about.'

'The German police seem to think the same. With the end of the war close, all the conquerors want is to get back to Germany.'

'De Graaf, who always has the latest news, said that the fire was no accident.'

'That wouldn't surprise anyone.'

The train I was waiting for finally showed itself in the distance and rolled into the station.

I held a copy of *Het Parool* newspaper as the agreed sign the woman would look for. A crowd got off the train and my attention was drawn to a beautifully dressed young woman, tall, brown hair, glowing skin. I let out a silent wolf whistle and sighed. My eyes continued to sweep across the tide of passengers surging towards me.

State of Guilt

I was looking for a plain solidly built German woman., but the woman I had noticed and admired, came straight towards me.

'Piet van Land?' She was as tall as I was in her slightly raised heels. She smiled showing white and even teeth .

'Uh – Inga Grutz?' I was stunned. She was exquisite. I took the hand she offered. Her handshake was firm and cool, while large, clear, light brown eyes looked steadily into mine.

She in no way resembled the podgy girl I had seen in Kurt's crumpled photograph. The round button nose had become straight over a generous, though not large mouth. The face, oval with a firm chin, was lightly tanned. Instead of presenting myself as suave and sophisticated, I felt awkward.

'Let me.' I broke the spell and took her small suitcase. 'Did you have a good journey?' Apart from a slight tremor, my voice sounded normal.

'I did, Piet. Were you able to get a room for me for the two nights?' she smiled again.

'Yes, I did.' I wondered if she felt my discomfort. 'It's just a short walk from here. Have you had something to eat?'

'I did have a sandwich on the train, thank you.'

I pointed to the exit and she walked slightly in front of me for some moments. Good figure. A cream-coloured jacket over a blue blouse and a straight navy blue skirt, just below the knee. No jewellery except small pearl earrings. If she wore make-up, in addition to the lipstick, it was not noticeable.

We collected the key from the hotel reception and she decided to go up to her room to freshen up. I tried to read my newspaper while I waited for her to come down. Inga reappeared, she had changed to a simple black dress with a single string of pearls.

It was late afternoon and I suggested a drink and then dinner.

Inga talked about her ambitions. She wanted to become a writer. 'I've had several poems published and hope to get enough poems together to publish my first volume.'

'That's wonderful.'

She smiled. 'A publisher has shown interest. He will need to choose at least sixty good poems, and I still have a lot of work to do before I have that many.'

Relaxing somewhat I told her about my photography and the hopes that I had of eventually starting my own business.

It wasn't long however before our conversation turned to Germany and the war.

'Let's not have any illusions.' I said. 'I honestly feel that what happened in Germany could have happened in almost any country under comparable circumstances. There was mass unemployment and galloping inflation. Most people didn't realise what the Nazis were doing. By the time they did, it was already too late.'

'As Germans, we can not forget what we did to the world.'

'You didn't, not you personally, Inga. After all, you were a child.'

'Yes, you might look at it like that, but many of us feel that we all share the guilt. After the war they made us watch films in school about the camps. The teachers felt it their duty to make us look over and over again at the mountains of skeletal corpses, skin and bones and so white! Thrown into heaps, like bracken. Arms and legs twisted, buttocks sticking out and faces, mouths open in horror over sunken cheeks and hollow staring eyes. It was like looking at Breughel's painting of hell. I will never forget those images.'

I took her hand, 'Don't accept those photographs as being representative of your life. The rise of the Nazis was not so extraordinary. Even in Holland the Nazis managed to persuade around twenty-five thousand men to join their armies. I remember that my own grandfather admired Hitler at one stage. Of course, all the silly old man talked about, knew about, was the Autobahnen. I suggest that not everyone in Germany fell for the clever propaganda.'

'Yes, there were those who disagreed with Nazism. Our own bishop of Münster did. He was a brave man who spoke out against the Nazi's policy of eugenics, the killing of mentally deficient people and of the long term unemployed. His courage failed him eventually because he didn't protest when the Jews and Gypsies were rounded up to be killed. Isn't that sad?' Her eyes became moist and her lips trembled for some moments.

'My father was in the army. I shudder to think that he might have been on the staff at one of the camps. Could he have been a party to the atrocities?'

'Give your father the benefit of the doubt.'

For an instant I saw Kurt again as he walked towards Mum but I pushed the image away.

'It helps to talk to you,' she smiled warmly. 'Kurt was different. He had hardly grown up. That's why I have to find out what happened to him. He was my big brother, and I loved him very much. He always protected me. I don't know how much Kurt knew. Father never talked to us about the war. He was always joking and laughing. As for Kurt, when they made him a soldier, he must have known that the war was already lost. That's why he deserted. By then the Allies were marching into Germany from one side and the Russians from the other.'

I touched Inga's hand again. 'I only knew your brother very briefly. I liked him. Kurt seemed a nice person,' I lied and hoped that his ghost was not lurking about somewhere, listening, or if he did, that he wouldn't be able to do anything to me apart from maybe sending me some nightmares, which I must create myself anyway.

She put her hand on mine. The light pressure of her fingertips sent a warm feeling through me.

'It's strange and wonderful', she said, 'that you, who must have hated us as the enemy, can make me feel so much better.'

My God, it went through my head: her brother has been buried by me only a short train ride away from here. I took a long sip of my excellent wine and felt it cool my throat. I put the glass down, I was going to concentrate entirely on Inga and look into her wonderful eyes. I did not want to be encumbered with further morbid thoughts about the war.

Inga could not let the subject go yet. 'I saw my father only at weekends and during his holidays. He was a nice man who brought us presents. I remember the perfume and delicious fois gras from Paris. He always looked strong, and very handsome in his uniform, the same uniform that now looks absurd, with its swastikas and eagles. I felt that we were a happy family. I remember the last few days we had together, all four of us, at home. That time it was different. Father was not his usual jovial self. No presents, no jokes. He was cold and distant, as if we were strangers. I don't know whether he had a premonition that he wouldn't come back. Maybe he volunteered or maybe he was sent to fight in Russia. He died there.'

'I'm sorry.'

'My mother never recovered from the shock of receiving the news of my father's death, and when Kurt had to go into the army as well, she said that she knew Kurt would not come back either. She gave up. I never saw her smile again. When the two men in her life had gone, she stopped caring. She finally died last year.'

'She still had you,' I said.

'I couldn't live with her. She still blamed everyone except the Nazi Party. We argued about that. She had to hang on to her beliefs. You see, if she had not, she would have had to concede that everything had been for nothing, that the life of her husband, her son, her own life, had been wasted. That would have been unthinkable. Their happiness and their suffering had all been for the Führer and the glory of the Fatherland. I never liked wearing uniforms, but we were made to join the Kindergruppe when we were six years old. All the girls had to be members of the *Jungmädelbund,* all part of the Hitler Youth. There were activities. You met children your own age to make friends with. We knew no other life.' She looked down into her glass.

At last she smiled, 'Thank you for this evening.'

'It was a pleasure.' I knew very well that just a few years ago, this woman, this German woman, beautiful as she was, would have been my worst enemy. That was irrelevant now as a warm feeling flooded through me, and I knew that I wanted to be close to her, know her. I felt that I understood and wanted to share her feelings. The fact that she was German didn't matter any more

* * *

After dinner I saw her walk across the hotel reception area to the lift. Then I was alone and it was as if I had awoken from a dream back to a reality that made me utterly miserable. God! The way she looked at me. How trusting she was. I had to struggle to meet her eyes. I turned and went into the café next door to the hotel. In quick succession I downed two jenevers. They didn't help. I went to my flat and sat down at the table.

In my mind I could hear Inga's soft voice and could see the tears welling up in her eyes. What I was doing to this woman was — were there any words to describe it? When I had been with her, I had stepped outside myself and had become someone else. Someone who had nothing to do with Kurt. The feelings of sympathy I felt for Inga had been real, and the opinions that I expressed to her had come naturally. However, was I being honest or was the whole evening a ploy to make this desirable woman like me? The only thing I was certain of was that I wanted to kiss her, caress her breasts and hold her body against mine.

I rubbed my forehead as I became aware of a blinding headache. I drank a large glass of water and swallowed three aspirins with it.

I needed to think and not let the right or wrong of Kurt's death come between us. She had accepted the official version of her brother's death. I had no right to take that away from her. It would be too cruel. If I could accept that Kurt had died in a fire as well, I would no longer have to feel guilty.

What really happened was no longer the truth. Memory could never be relied on. This new way of looking at Kurt's death had become the truth. The past had been recreated into a different kind of truth as it is in films and history books.

CHAPTER TWENTY-ONE

When I woke, my first thought was of Inga. This was immediately followed by the conviction that I had been foolish the previous night. I had talked too much. Now, in the sober morning light, I knew that I could not let myself get involved with this German woman. She was beautiful and there was no doubt that I was attracted to her and even if she liked me too, it was lunacy to consider that there could ever be anything between us. I would spend the day with her, as I had promised, then she must go back to Germany and forget me as I must forget her. I left home with my mind firmly made up.

Two minutes after I arrived at her hotel, the narrow lift door clattered open and Inga stepped out. Instantly my good intentions vanished. She looked radiant.

I went up to her and kissed her on the cheek. 'Good morning Inga. Did you sleep well?'

'Very well, Piet, although I had some very confusing dreams.'

I waited for her to continue.

'Kurt was with me, and we were young again. It was to be expected that I would dream about him now.'

During the short train ride to Hilversum we talked generalities. I pointed out features of the landscape as it flew past our window.

First we visited the building where I thought Kurt had been billeted. It was no longer a barracks and displayed a large sign: De Interact Assurantie B.V.

After that we walked to the house where the Police had told her Kurt had died. This was the difficult one for me, as I would have to encourage her to believe that everything she'd been told was true. A neat two-storeyed house that matched its neighbours had been erected where I only remembered a burnt-out shell.

'This is the place,' I said to her, trusting my face would not go crimson as I thought how the real grave of her brother was only a short walk away.

Inga took my arm and stood silent for a few minutes.

She turned. 'Thank you, Piet. At least now I know where Kurt died. It must have been horrible to die like that. So close, days away from peace. If it hadn't been for that accident he might have come back to us.'

I nodded and squeezed her arm. 'He made a statement by deserting. You have that.'

'Yes, I do. Thank you.'

The look she gave me showed such feelings of gratitude, that it made me want to shrink away to nothing. Instead I put my arms around her and held her. I kissed her smooth forehead and released her.

Our visit to the cemetery was brief. We found a wooden cross, about to fall over, that gave no names. It simply stated that the remains of two unknown German soldiers had been buried there in May 1945. Inga had bought flowers and laid them on the grave. She again stood still for a few minutes.

She asked me to find out from the caretaker if it was possible to have a stone cross with Kurt's name erected on the grave. Luckily he was nowhere to be found and I promised, rashly, that I would phone the cemetery later.

'Could we go back to Utrecht now?'

'Yes, we will be back there in time for lunch.' I was grateful to leave Hilversum. I wasn't certain if I could keep up the pretence much longer.

Inga said little during the train journey back to Utrecht and during lunch. Later we visited some shops and the Buurtkerk church, after which she asked to see some of my landscape photographs.

'The skies and the clouds are very strong. I can see that they are important to you,' Inga said.

'Yes, I try to capture the Dutch skies like so many of our painters did.'

It was five-thirty in the afternoon, and I thought she looked tired and I wasn't surprised when she said, 'I would like to go to my hotel now for an hour or so,' she said. 'Then tonight I insist on buying you dinner.'

During dinner we talked quietly and listened to the pianist who was playing in a corner of the restaurant. A few couples were dancing, and it crossed my mind that dancing with Inga would be delicious.

Instead, when we'd finished our dinner, she said, 'I hope you will understand that it's been a very emotional day for me. If you don't mind I would like to go back to the hotel.'

State of Guilt

'Of course not.' It was as if I woke from a lovely dream where it was be possible for us to be together 'Your train leaves at ten o'clock tomorrow morning, so I shall call for you at nine-thirty.'

'Could you make it nine again like this morning. I would like to have a little time with you before I leave.'

The next morning there was time for a leisurely coffee at the station.

'Has your coming here helped, Inga?'

'Yes, it has. I am going home knowing that Kurt is at rest, and I have seen where he spent his last few days. I thank you for being with me. It was difficult for me to come here, not knowing what I would find. I wasn't sure that I should or even wanted to come. Right up until the last minute, I was in two minds.'

'And now?'

'Now I'm glad I came. It has all meant so much to me. I'm also glad to have met you.'

For a moment I felt guilt flood through me again. I tried to ignore it. 'I hope your train journey home will be a pleasant one.'

'It will be, I'm sure. I have a lot to think about.'

The train was on the platform and all at once I was eager for her to leave, for me to get away. I felt uncomfortable and didn't quite know what to say to her any more. Except goodbye. We must never meet again. That was how it should be, despite the immensely strong attraction I felt for her. The guilt I felt about deceiving her was almost too much to bear. Now that I had met her, it would take forever to recover my peace of mind.

She stood at the door of the train as it was about to

depart and her brown eyes rested on me steadily. What was she thinking? Could she see into my mind?

'Well, goodbye, Piet, and thank you again for all you did for Kurt and for me.' She kissed me on the cheek.

I swallowed. 'It was nothing. So, bon voyage.'

She appeared at the open window of the train as it slowly began to move. 'I'll write to you,' she called and waved.

I wanted to call out: "Don't write. I don't want you to write. I never want to see you again. I can't; it's too difficult for me to cope with." Instead of that I nodded and waved back at her and watched the train pull out of the station until it disappeared round the curve in the track.

Back to work, I said to myself as I walked to the studio. I wanted to be busy and think only about work.

Inga, Inga. Your eyes, your face, the curve of your breasts as you leant forward while making a point. I want to be with you, even though I know that I must never ever see you again.

During the days following Inga's departure I found myself remembering the obvious rapport there had been between us. I wanted to see her again and ignored all the implications that I knew this would have. I also knew that I could not possibly expect anything to ever happen between us. There is still a choice, I told myself. Forget her smile. Act as if you've never met her. You can't follow your weak little heart that thinks it's in love.

Was I in love? I knew so clearly what I should be doing. Yet, I also knew that it was going to be difficult to dismiss her from my mind.

I could not decide whether I should be pleased that I

had met Inga or curse the day I sent Kurt's papers back. Writing my address on the reverse side had been habit, but that habit had made certain that there would be contact. I had allowed myself to have feelings for Inga knowing that there could not be a future for us. Sooner or later, the truth about her brother's death would come out. Then what? In addition I would constantly be reminded of him if I allowed myself to become involved with Inga.

Yet there also was that voice telling me that Kurt would never be discovered. Why should he be found? So should I forfeit my chance of happiness for a "might happen"? Doesn't the world belong to the bold? Why shouldn't I grab my happiness when it was presenting itself to me? Inga was the most beautiful woman I had ever met and so utterly different from Kurt that being with her could not possibly remind me of him.

You're mad, I'd say then. You're complicating your life in a most stupid, reckless way. What's so special about this woman? There are plenty of sexy, attractive Dutch girls, and two or three of the ones you know are interested in you right now. All you have to do is call them.

So I struggled on throughout the week that followed her visit, swinging from exhilaration when I planned to see her again, to deep depression.

Her letter came as I knew it would. Burn it! Was my first thought. Don't open it. Burn it now. Yet I knew I would open that letter. I had to. I was like a soldier who gets a command that is so dangerous that following it, will certainly lead to his death but who does so, knowing this.

The letter was headed "Dear Piet," and she signed it, "Love, Inga." That made me happy. Nevertheless, I decided to be strong and not answer her letter. I lasted two weeks. Then a postcard from Münster arrived. It showed the cathedral where the brave cardinal Von Galen had been bishop from 1933 to 1946 when he died. The message on the reverse of the card simply said, "Only to say hello."

This was too much for me. This brief message overcame all my objections and fears about the consequences. Yes, I wanted to see her again and I knew I would do anything to make it happen.

I wrote four pages that night. I held the letter in the slot of the letterbox, wavering, knowing that I'd shown my feelings for her, at the same time thinking that this was foolish.

Someone was standing behind me, obviously waiting to post a letter too. It prompted me to let go of my letter. So I sealed my fate.

I knew then that Inga and I would become lovers. It excited me as much as it scared me. I couldn't deny that I was immensely attracted to her. The problem was how was I going to keep Kurt from coming between us? The dreams were still with me. Whenever I thought I was free of them, bang, there he was again, just as ugly as ever, slashing at me with his knife. The nightmares might even give me away and I would constantly need to be vigilant to stop the occasional word from slipping out. If I knew it could all turn out bad, I also believed that we should grab every opportunity for happiness as it comes along even if there are great risks, because if you didn't, you would certainly lose out, or as Mum used to say, you've got a no already and you might get a yes.

I reminded myself of the fact that I'd never wanted

Kurt's death. I had been a mere bystander, guilty by association only. After all, there were degrees of guilt, and mine was of a very much lesser kind. Yes, I felt guilty about my part in the murder and I hated the feeling, I didn't want to feel like this and I was determined to fight it.

CHAPTER TWENTY-TWO

Dear Piet,
Your letter has made me happy. I had hoped that you would write, but I would not have blamed you if you had not. I have decided to introduce you by letter to my dear Aunt Elsa. She is my mother's younger sister and only eight years older than myself, so we are really more like sisters.

Before the war Aunt Elsa was a promising young mezzo-soprano, and lived in Berlin. When her singing teacher, who was half Jewish, was replaced by one who did not object to arranging performances for Nazi gatherings, Aunt Elsa developed a permanent throat condition.

I have always idealised her and when she came home to Münster after the war I was so very pleased, as she is the only relative I have left. We see each other once a week, that is, when she is not away singing, and we have spent many holidays together.

As you can imagine, I am very proud of her. She

State of Guilt

has introduced me to many musicians, whom I never would have met, had she not been my aunt. I hope that one day soon you will meet her and hear her sing.

Inga's letter went on to describe Münster and she signed again, "With Love". It made me feel a little light-headed as well as making me aware of the negative thoughts that lurked at the edge of my consciousness. I told myself, 'This is dangerous, you fool.' The letter sounded almost like an invitation. There was no turning back now. I should have known better, and although I *did* know better, I didn't care. I wanted to see her again, be with her. I pushed everything else aside.

Then there it was. Come to Münster for a weekend. Aunt Elsa would be staying with Inga so I could meet her at the same time.

During the war, we'd all sworn that we would never set foot in Germany and had meant it. That was then. If I hadn't met Inga I'd probably have stuck to that oath. This was different. Inga was there, beautiful, tall, slim, sophisticated Inga. How could I refuse an invitation from her? German or not German.

Münster was a surprise. As I drove into the small university town at mid-morning I noticed it was not so different from some of the older Dutch towns.

Number forty-eight Cramerstrasse was a quiet street away from the centre. Inga's two storeyed house was painted a light yellow ochre with white windows and shutters. The square red-tiled building was surrounded by an established garden. It was almost spring and the early flowers were showing their colours in the crisp air.

I arrived in the late afternoon and the sunlight was soft and golden. I was pleased to see a bed of bright red and yellow tulips.

I walked up the front door and pressed the bell.

'Welcome to Münster.' Inga was wearing a white polo neck sweater and dark blue slacks.

'It's lovely, Inga. Münster is a lovely town and what a lovely house and how lovely you look.'

'You look well, too, Piet. Obviously the drive was not too exhausting?'

'Perfect. It only took about three hours.'

'Come inside and meet my aunt Elsa.'

The entrance hall was wide. I noticed several paintings and a grandfather clock. The door to the living area was open and a woman of around forty faced us. She took a few steps towards me offering her hand.

'So this is Piet.'

It was a statement. Blue-grey eyes looked into mine. I wondered how deep aunt Elsa could look into me. What did she see? Did she like me? Not that she wasn't welcoming. The smile was warm and genuine but there was something else that made me feel slightly uncomfortable.

'You must promise me one thing, Piet.'

'Which is?'

'You must never ever think of me as Inga's aunt.'

'How could I? You're much too young to be an aunt.'

After a simple lunch Inga took me to the Prinzipalmarkt where the houses had high stepped gables. We passed the Lamberti church and Inga pointed out the iron cages on the wall.

'Those cages are a reminder of the revolt against the Anabaptists.'

'Anabaptists, they were a religious group, weren't they?'

'Yes they were a group of Protestants who had their own ideas about how life should be lived. The movement started in Zürich and quickly spread through Switzerland, Germany and especially your country.'

'I thought I'd heard of them.'

'Hundreds of Dutch Anabaptists came to Münster to join local groups. They took over the city to create a new Jerusalem. Anyone who refused to be baptised by them was banished from the city.'

'Love thy neighbour, uh?'

'Yes. In 1536 the population decided they'd had enough and started executing the Anabaptists. Some were put in those cages, left to die.'

* * *

For the evening Inga had booked seats for a concert at the cathedral, damaged during the war but beautifully restored. Aunt Elsa was singing. She wasn't a tall woman, but she had an amazingly powerful voice that filled the whole ancient building. She earned my instant admiration by performing Bach's *Erbarme Dich,* from the *St. Matthew Passion,* one of my favourite works.

After the concert we went for a meal with friends and admirers of Aunt Elsa and Inga, and I was surprised that I didn't mind meeting all those perfectly pleasant Germans. I was even glad that I could follow most of the conversations around me.

Inga stood up and said, 'I thought we might have a short walk along the water before we go home.'

I nodded, pleased, as despite the happy atmosphere in the restaurant, I looked forward to being alone with Inga. I saw Elsa wave at us. 'You go along. Helmut will look after me.' She patted the hand of the young man sitting next to her.

'*Natürlich.*' He happily put his arm around Elsa's waist.

Outside walking along the deserted street, Inga took my arm. 'I hope you have enjoyed the concert and meeting all those noisy Germans.'

'I certainly did. What a voice Elsa has, and the food and the beer. Thank you for arranging today,' I said. 'It was wonderful. I like being in your city and meeting your friends. I want to know everything about you. Absolutely everything.'

'You shall. And I want to know everything about you, too.'

'There is not much to know.'

'I don't believe that.'

I stopped, pulled her close and kissed her.

We started walking again and soon reached her house. Inside the front door Inga turned the key in the lock and slid the bolt home.

'What about Elsa?'

'She will go to her own flat.'

CHAPTER TWENTY-THREE

Inga and I enjoyed the late spring sunshine, out of the soft breeze, having coffee on the glassed-in terrace of the Hotel Centraal in Utrecht. Across the street, on the cobbled square, the weekly market was in progress. The square was bordered by tall houses. On the sunny side was the light airy mood, while in the shade the buildings looked more serious.

People, some young, some surprisingly old, sailed past on their heavy Dutch bicycles. A number of bikes had parcels tied to them, others had cane basket seats behind the saddle, in which blond children sat calmly surveying the world with big blue eyes.

In the market, a small crowd moved slowly from stall to stall. Women bunched around a stall loaded with assorted cheeses. Heavy overcoats had been left at home. Summer was nearly here and, with the sun, bright colours were back.

Inga and I were content to feel the warmth of the sun on our faces and watch the scene in front of us while we sipped our coffee. I glanced at Inga and smiled. Her skin seemed to glow from within and the sun was playing games with the darkness of her hair, saying, "Let me show you some of the colours that you had not noticed before."

Her eyes were bright as she turned to me and said, casually, 'If I tried, I could easily live here.'

I did not answer at once, but a warm feeling spread through me. Then I said, 'That's wonderful to know.'

We had been seeing each other frequently at weekends. Some weekends Inga came and stayed with me. She loved the old part of Utrecht and had insisted on climbing the four hundred and sixty-five steps to the top of the Dom Tower.

When she mentioned living in Holland, I felt that she had already made up her mind. While we said no more about it that day, all through the next week I could think of little else.

After losing Anja I had felt that marriage and cohabitation would never be for me, sharing an apartment, bathroom, everything, but this was different. I had loved Anja with her touch of madness and on my part it had been an obsessive love. I had needed Anja, much more than she had needed me.

With Inga I did not feel anxious when we were apart. I knew she loved me in the same way I loved her. We both, I thought, wanted to be together, and the happiness we felt in each other's company stayed with us when we were apart.

The guilt I carried with me about Inga's brother, had been relegated to the past and had been replaced by my lust for total possession of her. Guilt was over and done with. Live for the present, for today. I did not want to think about it any more, not now. "Let her love you. Don't let her go. You will never feel like this again." To have her body next to mine every night was the ultimate wish fulfillment.

The next weekend I told her that I loved her very much and asked if she would come and live with me.

'Shall we think about it very carefully? It's something we should not go into lightly.' She kissed my naked shoulder. 'I do love you.'

We talked about the practicalities of living together, about money and her work.

'Money is no problem,' I said, 'and because you work only two days a week as an editorial assistant at present, there will be few professional ties to be cut. Your collection of poetry is almost finished and you can continue writing while living in Holland.'

The following Thursday night she telephoned. 'Come and get me.'

'Yes, yes, yes!' I called into the phone.

Inga laughed. 'Not so loud.'

'I'm sorry, darling. I got a little excited. You've made me a very happy man. I'll be there tomorrow.'

It was true, I was excited. I could hardly sit still, planning, making wardrobe space available for her, tidying the place and cleaning like a Dutch housewife at springtime. I took the Friday off and drove up to Inga's house in record time.

I'd brought some empty suitcases and while Inga was folding frocks and blouses, I decided to help and pack some clothes for her. She opened the heavy carved doors of the big wardrobe. I emptied the top shelf and put the clothes on the bed for Inga to sort. I stepped back and just managed to catch the object that came flying off the shelf with the jumpers. It was a very small handgun. Beautifully made with ivory set into its silver grip.

'Wow!' I called out. 'What a lovely gun.'

Inga came over. 'Oh, that. I'd forgotten about that thing. It was my mother's.'

She reached out and I handed it to her. She put the gun back on the top shelf of the wardrobe.

'My mother told me that father had given it to her. It was a war trophy from somewhere, France I think. Both she and Father were totally convinced that the Russians would overrun all of Germany and all of Western Europe. When that happened she was to use the gun on me and on herself.' She smiled. 'Poor Mum. She became obsessed with the threat of the Russians. There were many stories of atrocities committed by the occupying troops, and she told them over and over again.'

Inga's mother hadn't been alone in dreading the Russians. I had read that a large percentage of the immigrants who left Holland after the war did so because of the "Red Threat". The general opinion was that the Russians would not stop advancing until they reached the North Sea.

'That's all.' She snapped the suitcases shut. 'Let's leave it at this for the moment. If I need to get more of anything, we'll have a good excuse to spend a weekend here.'

'I'd like that,' I said. 'I look forward to photographing Münster.'

I'd always thought of myself as being quite tidy and of having reasonable taste. After Inga had moved in I was not so sure. In a few weeks she transformed my rather Spartan flat into a wonderful home. Out with the tired old sofa that I'd inherited from a previous tenant. In came a new one, cream upholstered. You could sit on this one anywhere at all without getting stabbed in the buttocks by aggressive springs. She'd had the living room repapered in a predominantly pale yellow. Two of her own paintings by a German artist hung on one wall. The rest of the room showed six of my best black and white photographs.

Later that year Richard Oosterdaal decided that he wanted to retire. I jumped at the chance of taking over the business. When, not long after this, the assistant who had come with the business decided to leave, Inga at once suggested that she fill the vacancy.

She already spoke French and English, and soon spoke Dutch with only a very slight accent. As time went by this became even less pronounced. Nothing pleased her more than someone asking her what part of Holland she came from.

Most people don't like having their photograph taken, for reasons I've never quite understood. One theory is that your soul will be taken from you when the shutter clicks shut. Another is that the camera makes people uncomfortable because the lens is like an eye watching you, and you can't have eye contact with a piece of glass; it's impersonal, all-seeing, threatening.

Whatever the cause of people's unease or embarrassment, Inga had the gift of making our clients feel relaxed. She loved being with people and they enjoyed having her fuss over them.

Some days we had to cope with difficult clients. 'I don't like it here,' was the first thing the daughter had said. It took Inga ten minutes to remove the scowl from the eight year old's face, and even then I wondered whether her little face had not reverted back to its original countenance at the precise moment I pressed the shutter.

As we turned the "Open" sign on the shop door to "Closed", Inga said to me, 'You ought to do more landscapes. I feel it would make you happier than photographing babies and doing family portraits.'

CHAPTER TWENTY-FOUR

Whenever the capricious Dutch weather and the volume of work allowed me to do so, I started to go out very early two or three mornings a week. It was sheer happiness waiting for the sun to come up and watch the landscape slowly being flooded with soft morning light towards the perfect moment to take the picture.

Back at the studio at around ten or eleven, I disappeared into the darkroom. Once I'd developed the film and printed a contact sheet, Inga and I poured over the images with a viewer, marking the ones we felt merited printing. Looking at the prints, she would half-close her eyes and touch her earlobe, giving it a gentle rub, then make her comments. I generally agreed with her opinion.

The day arrived when we decided to see how many of my photographs would be suitable for an exhibition. I slapped the large portfolio that held my best work on the table, opened it and took out the first of the twenty-five by forty centimeter prints. We looked at them with a super critical eye. As I handed her the last of the large prints a smaller one, half the size of the others, was left behind.

It was an image that I had bought from the newspaper where it had been published shortly after the war had ended.

Inga took the photograph. 'What is this, Piet? What a horrible picture. The girl looks so unhappy.'

'Oh, that. Yes, she does look terrible, doesn't she? It was going to be one of my projects. She is a girl who had the misfortune to fall in love with a German soldier. After the war her hair was hacked off by a mob of so-called patriots that seemed to spring up out of nowhere. She was paraded through crowds of men and women yelling at her, "Slut! Whore," and whatever else they could think of.'

Inga stared at the photograph, eyes wide and forehead wrinkled. She shook her head. 'Barbaric.'

'It was. That was one of the reasons why I kept the photograph, to remind me of that aspect of the war. I wanted to do a series of images starting with a portrait of a lovely girl with her full head of hair. Then a picture of her with her hair like the one you're looking at now. After that a series of portraits as her hair slowly grows back, signifying how she gradually becomes able to cope with the memory of that terrifying experience. The last photograph was to show her with a full head of hair once again, a year later, or whatever time it took.'

'That's a worthwhile project,' Inga said.

'At the time I felt that nobody had the right to judge anyone and I still do. If she happened to fall in love with a German, it was nobody else's business. I wanted to show that she was perfectly human and I hoped, that it might make people realise the horror of the treatment and how wrong it had been.'

Inga nodded. 'It would be as important as your landscapes.'

'I was planning to do it after I came out of the army. I thought it would give direction to my career. I even found the girl in the picture who'd undergone "the treatment". After talking to her for some time, explaining what I wanted to do, she agreed to pose for me.'

'Well? Why didn't you do it then?'

'Because she changed her mind. She said talking about it had brought back all the violence of the experience. She'd moved to another town and made a new life for herself. If she agreed to pose for me, people might recognise her and start harassing her. I understood; as I knew how self-righteous people can be. I tried to get professional models to pose for me using theatrical wigs and make-up and I couldn't find anyone willing to play the role of a Dutch girlfriend of a German soldier. So I shelved the project.'

'That's a pity,' Inga said.

We continued to look at the landscape photographs, selecting only the best ones. Before we started to sort the prints, there were about forty of them. I'd felt that the time for finding a gallery space was getting close. As print after print was rejected, I began to feel that instead of weeks away, it seemed more like months, or even a year.

'They should all be of this quality, Piet.'

She pointed at the ebb-tide picture that I'd taken on the island of Terschelling. I'd been tramping around the island all of a sunny September day looking for the ultimate sand-dune shot. After carrying equipment for hours, it becomes heavy, and I had given up trying to get anything outstanding for the day. My body was tired and my throat felt as if I'd swallowed half a tin of baby powder. I was thinking of a nice cold beer or two as I came back into the township of West-Terschelling, where I'd taken a room for four days. The sun was huge and on its way down. I decided to go up to the lookout. It was an excuse for a hill, about ten metres high. As it was the highest point on the island, there was always someone up there looking out to sea, keeping the granite statue of the squat fisherman's widow company as she, hand over her stony eyes, searched the horizon for her never to return husband.

I'd taken sunset shots up there a few days earlier, and had some acceptable images. That late afternoon the tide was very low. I gasped as I stepped off the concrete stairs onto the grassed top of the small mount. The water on that side of the island, away from the harbour, is quite shallow and as I looked out into the setting sun, the exposed sand stretched out for what seemed forever. There were many gullies filled with water running across my field of vision on the wet, gleaming sand-flats. Each one of the narrow channels reflected the cloudless sky with a brilliant slice of a huge red sun right in the centre. I'd never seen the sun reflected so many times, and so powerfully.

My fingers trembled with excitement as I set up my tripod, my tiredness completely gone. I knew I was looking at the shot of a lifetime. I managed to shoot off three rolls with various focal length lenses, bracketing the exposure times like mad, to make quite certain that I would capture the incredible scene perfectly. So yes, Inga was right again, I admitted as I closed the folder.

The print of the girl was still lying on the table. Inga picked it up. 'Why don't you have another try at the girl series?'

I wasn't sure. 'It's probably not of interest any more. People want to forget the war.'

She shook her head. 'Horror like this is never out of date. Perhaps the girl, who is older now, might agree today. It would make a powerful exhibition if you could show such a series of photographs besides your landscapes, wouldn't it?'

I held the picture and looking at it was again struck by the desperate, haunted look in the girl's eyes. Her face scrunched up with fear. 'I could try once more. The girl's name was Andrea.'

* * *

I still had Andrea's address and she answered at once when I called her.

'I'll think about it,' was all she would promise. 'I'll let you know.'

Her call came the following day. 'I'm married now. My husband knows what I went through and he strongly objects to my having anything to do with that project.'

'That's a pity,' I said. 'I understand.'

'You can't blame her', Inga said, 'It's the one day of her life that she wants to forget. It's still been nice to get enthusiastic about the project for a while.'

'Yes. Well, as a consolation, I'll go and take some photographs of Delft tomorrow. That's been on my programme for some time. I've always loved the way in which Vermeer painted light and dark in his city. It'll be a challenge to find a little corner to attempt to record that on film.'

'You must take me there soon. You've made me want to see it now.'

After I had promised, she continued, 'This afternoon,

we don't have a full book, so could we take the photographs of both of us that we promised Elsa weeks ago. She's been so good to us, and she doesn't have a recent photograph of me. Will you be able to make the time? One of me and I can take one of you,' she smiled, 'as long as you show me where the shutter is.'

'Of course. I'm sure you'll manage. We'll send her a nice selection of you and one of me. Nobody wants to clutter up their albums with too many pictures of me.'

CHAPTER TWENTY-FIVE

On Monday mornings, in common with most high street businesses, we didn't open our doors until one o'clock. It was another opportunity for me go out in search of images. I returned home at around eleven, happy as I was certain I had taken one or two good shots.

Inga was in the kitchen. She turned to greet me. 'A nice fresh coffee?'

'Yes please, I'd love one.' I said and put my arms around her and kissed her, breathing in her perfume. I sat down on one of the kitchen chairs and asked her, 'Did you have a relaxed morning?'

'Oh yes, I did,' she said. 'I slept in a little, did some shopping, very successful. Then met my friend Tina for a chat.'

I wanted to tell her about my morning, when I noticed that there was something different about Inga. I looked at her closely and then I saw it. 'What have you done with your hair? Have you had it cut, trimmed or is it simply a new style?'

She put the coffee on the table, smiling mysteriously

and, stepping back slowly to the sideboard, she picked up the biscuit tin. I was watching her intently, trying to determine what exactly was different about her. She let me take a biscuit. 'Your favourites.'

'Mmm, thank you.' I bit into the sugary biscuit covered with dark chocolate and picked up my coffee.

She shook her head sideways as she often did to swing her hair off her face. Still smiling.

I laughed. 'Come on, you've made me curious now. What have you done that's different?'

'Well, promise me that you won't be shocked. You love me as I am, right?'

'You know I do. I love you for ever and more than I thought possible.'

'That's good, because I'm about to test your love.'

Test my love? I felt panic. I immediately feared that she'd found out how her brother had died. I relaxed, it had to be something else or she most certainly wouldn't be so light-hearted.

She stood in front of me, looking down as I took a sip of my coffee. 'Do you remember how you found it impossible to get anyone to pose for the series of photographs you'd planned of the Dutch girl with the German boyfriend?'

'Of course, I do. What does that have to do with the way you look?'

'Well, you can take those pictures now. I am going to be your model. You already have great photos of me with all my hair. If you want to make the series look really dramatic, you could print a picture of a German soldier in uniform in the background.'

Still smiling, she put her hand to her hair and to my

horror she pulled at it and it came off in her hand. She'd been wearing a wig! Her own hair had been hacked off just like the girl in the picture.

'No, Inga, no!' I jumped up and my cup dropped to the floor. I could feel the hot coffee burn my leg as it splashed down my trousers. I grabbed her by the shoulders, wanting to block out what I saw. 'Why, why did you do this!? It's – it's –'

'Because I love you. I did it because I want you to take those pictures. I believe in them and I feel they're important. I want you to do it for yourself, for everyone and for all the people who suffered during the war. What happened to that girl Andrea was horrible, and I want to make a statement by playing my part in protesting against it – most of all for my brother Kurt. I feel so much closer to him here in Holland. I want to do it to make people see that hatred and revenge have no place in a civilised world.'

Her eyes were glowing and her smile was brilliant, 'Is it horrible, do I look very ugly?'

I was looking at Inga and I saw Kurt's face. I tried to fight back my tears as they rushed from my eyes, unstoppable. They'd been building up for a long time. The more I loved Inga and the more she loved me, the more the misery of my guilt brimmed at the edge of my consciousness. So far I'd managed to keep control of it.

I cried for Kurt who had to die and for Anja who felt she had to kill him, and I also cried for myself but most of all I cried for Inga. If the truth should ever be uncovered it would devastate her. I was in the middle of it all without having planned to be there. I felt hysterical, and was unable to stop my shaking body.

'Poor Piet, you're so sensitive. That's why I love you so much.' She put her arms around me.

I closed my eyes tightly, trying to shut Kurt out of my mind and remember that I was a man now. Experienced and in control I was not because I couldn't stop sobbing. This sudden evidence of the immensity of her love had completely overwhelmed me. She held me close and stroked my head. At long last I felt my pain subside. I began to breathe deeply and became calmer. Still, I could not look at her. I'd betrayed her in a most despicable way. She was wasting her love on me and I couldn't tell her so. How could I have let it go this far? At that moment I experienced such regret and misery, it told me that I would never be at peace with myself.

'Better?'

I nodded dumbly, because Inga expected it from me. If only ... if only I could tell her, and look into her eyes without guilt. I never expected her to do this for me. And I never thought that I would allow myself to feel such love for anyone and at the same time to be so utterly devastated by it. I knew that Inga could never love me and forgive me if she knew the whole truth. Nobody could take that much betrayal. If only I'd told her at the very beginning what had really happened to her brother. Then she might have rejected me, hated me, but eventually she might have been able to forgive me. Even if she hadn't, at least I would have been able to live with myself; it would have been clean, like saving your life by cutting off a limb that is rotting with gangrene and threatening to poison your whole body.

It was Inga's right to see justice done, even if it might hurt Anja. The happiness that I'd waited for for so long was

State of Guilt

based on lies. It was too fragile for me to enjoy because I knew how easily it could be destroyed. I was in the middle of a minefield. At any moment, at any step, it might all explode and blow my life away.

'Do you find me too ugly to look at now?'

I shook my head. 'Of course not. It's just –'

Her lips were inviting and I responded, feeling her body hard against mine. What could I do? Kill myself? I thought of Inga's little hand gun on the top shelf of her wardrobe in Münster and knew that I'd never have the courage to pull the tiny trigger.

Inga led me to the bedroom and even though I hated myself, before long, all my dark thoughts evaporated and I soon wondered why I had cried. Everything was beautiful.

I kissed her hands and she took my head and placed it between her breasts. I kissed both of them and looked up into her eyes, 'Oh, I do love you so much.' I really meant that more than anything I'd ever said.

'I love you too, Piet. You know that now, don't you?'

'I do, Inga. I do.'

I kissed her breasts again and thought how wonderful it would be if we were to have a child together. I wanted to tell her and sat up. 'Inga …'

'Hush,' she put a finger on her lips and pulled me on top of her. 'Later.'

Our lovemaking was slow and I felt a great tenderness towards her and gratefulness for her love for me. This was such a new experience for me that it was as if we were making love for the first time.

As we lay silent, I hoped that Inga might have forgotten

to take her pill, as she had done on several occasions, so she had told me. Then we might have a child together.

*　*　*

Doing something that you feel is terribly wrong and cruel, something you despise yourself for, is difficult to live with, but once it's done and you know that there is no way back, you have to learn to live with it. Though despair had permeated every facet of my life, like a putrid smell will penetrate every corner of a room, I could only continue to live and love the best way I could.

Some days, I suddenly, without warning, felt so ashamed and uncomfortable that my heart would start to beat madly and beads of sweat would form on my upper lip. Then I could hardly look at Inga. It was her love and trust that had made her leave home and country to come to Holland to be with me.

By cutting off her hair she was proving that she was fully intent on sharing my life and work to the full. If she hadn't loved me so much, so unconditionally, it would have been easier for me. I asked myself, how far will I go? I was worse, far worse than the mob that had chased Kurt and would have killed him or even the mob that cut off the girl collaborator's hair. At least they had been honest about their hatred, whereas I was pretending to be what I was not. I knew it only too well. Yet I couldn't change anything now. I'd locked myself into a mental prison of my own making with a life sentence.

The wig she had managed to buy was excellent. It matched her hair perfectly. She had nearly fooled me and none of our friends or clients ever noticed. At night or when we were alone together she took the wig off. It was, she said, so I could get the full impact of the dreadful act

State of Guilt

of punishment that was handed out to the girls that dared to have Germans as lovers.

It seemed astonishing that even for a moment, when she had first removed her wig, I could have seen her brother's face in Inga's. It must have been a trick of the light that at a certain angle, had picked out and magnified similarities in facial structure. I never saw that again. With her short hair, Inga looked erotic in a different way, younger, and with her slim hips and her small, high breasts, like a boy Adonis who is almost too beautiful. Every time I looked at her I wanted her, and we made love every night and often again in the morning.

I loved her more each day and it was during that time that I first began to think of marriage. That Inga was committed to our relationship was without doubt. What about me I thought? Was I ready to commit myself fully to her? Was it possible that with my guilt and self-disgust I could dare to consider marriage and even children? Once the idea had arisen, it slowly firmed in my mind, and soon I knew that I was going to act on it. After all, her brother was safely buried and I thought how much I would regret not having married Inga when we'd both grown old and Kurt's grave had never been discovered.

We took a range of photographs of Inga as she was with her hair hacked off. It was to be the first photograph in the series. We experimented with different make-up and facial expressions. Finally we decided on the shot that portrayed the horror of the girl to our satisfaction. We then had one session a month to take the photograph that would show the growth of Inga's hair. I printed an image of a German soldier in the background, making this each month a little less distinct, showing how the girl

Johannes Kerkhoven

was letting go of her past as the German faded out of her life. After six months, he had completely disappeared.

Inga's thick hair grew quite quickly to a more generally acceptable length and soon it was time to discard the wig.

We wanted to make a little ceremony of it, so we decided to burn it. We drove to Spaanders Forest, which I knew well from my wood-cutting days during the war and found a secluded spot. We felt that burning the wig was symbolic and we made a wish that the horrors of war would disappear with it. We would have had second thoughts about burning it if we had known the awful smell it would give off.

As we walked back to the car, sunlight was filtering through the tightly packed tops of the huge beech trees standing on each side of the path. I stopped and looked up. 'This is wonderful.'

Inga's hand was in mine, cool and slim. We walked along slowly, not talking for some time. I no longer wanted to consider the possibility of our love ever ending for whatever reason. At that moment, even my guilt was no longer important. I looked into her eyes. She smiled at me, a question in her eyes.

I knelt on one knee, and then couldn't think of all I had planned to say. So I simply said , 'Inga, will you marry me?'

For some moments she said nothing. She shook her head. 'Piet, I was beginning to think that I would have to ask you.'

'Thank heavens for that.' I got up. 'This beech nut under my knee is giving me hell.' I held it up and rubbed my leg vigorously. 'Another few seconds and my kneecap would have split in two.'

We held each other silently.

CHAPTER TWENTY-SIX

Inga wanted to get married in Germany and I readily agreed. To give us time to make arrangements we decided to put our wedding date back a little.

In the meantime we concentrated on finishing the portraits of the "Girl Series". We'd tried to show Inga's face more relaxed each month, until finally after ten months, her hair had almost grown back to its original length. In the last photograph I took, Inga was smiling brilliantly and looked so happy, that we felt the series was complete. We discussed taking further pictures, showing the girl married with a child. This didn't seem necessary any more. The final picture showed a woman who had regained her life and self-esteem.

Gallerie Fotografiek was getting impatient. They'd already accepted my collection of landscapes and were pressing me to deliver the "Girl Series" as the time to the opening date was suddenly getting uncomfortably close.

The framing of the "Girl Series" was completed one day ahead of the opening of the exhibition. It was my first showing and I was totally unknown, so there was no press

State of Guilt

coverage. Yet three prints of the Terschelling sunset shot were sold on the opening day.

Life was perfect. I was going to marry the woman I loved and this, together with seeing my photographs on the wall, was pure happiness.

To keep up the creative feeling, I decided to take more photographs and drive to Naarden. I planned to let my inspiration guide me as to what subject I would take. The town's defenses are built in the pattern of a star and are claimed, by the good burghers of Naarden, to be the world's most perfectly preserved fortifications. As I walked around the outside of the walls, I enjoyed seeing their red, yellow and orange bricks and sloping grass tops reflected in the still moat around them. I'd visited Naarden years before with my school and I remembered dark tunnels and gloomy rooms and knew there would be interesting images waiting for me to click my shutter on. The day was brilliant with that cool, clear air that shows off the blue of the sky twice as deep as it might be on a day that might appear clear, but has a slight haze.

I took pictures from every angle. In most of them the square tower of the church with its short spire showed above the trees. I went inside the building and managed to get a good shot of the main stained glass window and a glowing picture of the immense organ.

Although I knew that one can never be sure of anything until the film is developed and you are watching the image form on the blank piece of paper in the tray of developer, I felt that I might have some useful shots in the fifteen or so rolls I'd exposed. Maybe even one great one.

I glanced at my watch and decided to head for home.

I would be in time for lunch, always something to look forward to with Inga, whether at home or out. After lunch, if no unexpected customers turned up, I planned to develop my films and print up the contact sheets.

CHAPTER TWENTY-SEVEN

Inga was standing by the door when I entered. My mouth opened to speak when I saw that she looked pale and ill. Something was very wrong. I was concerned. 'What is it? What's happened?'

She didn't answer and as I approached her she stepped aside and turned away from my kiss. She thrust a newspaper at me.

The next second my eyes took in the headline. "SKELETON FOUND IN GARDEN."

Kurt! I felt as if I was struck on the head and for some eternal seconds everything went black. I stumbled and held on to the doorpost. My brain raced as I tried to steady myself and read the dancing words. 'The body of a young man, aged around eighteen …'

'Tell me this has nothing to do with you, Piet, nothing at all.' Her voice was trembling.

'I …'

'It *is* Kurt, isn't it?' Her voice cut through me like cold steel.

My eyes were stuck again on the headline. I did not

have to read all of the story. My eyes moved down, reading a word here and there. It named the street where Mum and Dad still lived. "New owner digs up body".

Tears welled up in her beautiful eyes. I wanted to kiss them away – tell her everything. As I tried to speak words would not come. I was stunned, frozen. I could only stare at her. I was in shock, incapacitated by the straightjacket of guilt.

She picked up the suitcase that I hadn't noticed before. She'd been so sure that the skeleton was that of her brother, that she had packed and was ready to go. My whole being was stunned into a state if immobility. I knew that this by itself was as damning as if I'd handed Inga a written and signed statement of my guilt.

'Why did you send my brother's papers to me and why did you let me fall in love with you? Are you any better than the Nazis?'

I knew I had to speak, say something. 'Inga … It's not what you think. There was an accident …' I began. I desperately wanted to explain, but even then knowing that I would not be able to make her believe me, not now, not ever. The wrong that I had done to her could never be undone.

'I can see it in your face, Piet. Now I know how Kurt died. There is no need for you to say anything. You killed him. My God, to think that I loved you.'

She put a hand to her forehead, and the suitcase slipped from her hand. I thought she was going to faint and took a step towards her.

'No. Don't come near me.'

I stood there paralysed, looking at her, my eyes begging as I felt my life slipping away from me. It was as

State of Guilt

if my heart was being ripped out, and I was helpless. There was nothing I could possibly say or do that would undo this moment or would make any difference. What was left of my life was being decided right this very minute and I had absolutely no control over it.

She straightened herself and, shaking her head, picked up the suitcase again and walked to the door. 'Is this your revenge on the Germans? For three years you have lived this despicable lie. You made me believe that my brother had died in a fire, and even pretended that you had helped him.'

The front door clicked shut behind her and closed with a finality that left no hope. I wanted to follow her, talk to her, beg her to listen and tell her that I had never wanted Kurt to die. I could think of nothing I might say that could undo the past.

My hand was shaking as I opened the door and watched her walking out of my life. I ran after her, desperate. 'Inga, Inga, I love you so much. Please, please, listen to me.'

She did not stop walking or even look at me.

'Inga, please give me one minute, sixty seconds. I can't live without you – please.'

She stopped then, still looking at some point in the distance.

'I wanted to help Kurt,' I said. 'He didn't understand what I said to him in German. He – he attacked me with an axe and – '

She turned and looked at me.

'He walked into the knife I was holding. I didn't want him to die, Inga, I did *not*.'

'Even if that were true, you still made me believe that

he died in a fire and you even showed me the grave where his ashes were buried, while you knew all the time where his grave really was. Where you buried him. You did, didn't you. How could you?'

'I was so much in love with you that I felt if I told you the truth you would want nothing to do with me.'

'Well, I don't now. Our relationship was a lie.' She had not looked at me. 'Your minute is up, so please don't bother me again, ever.'

I still wanted to run after her, stop her as she walked away. The guilt overwhelmed me. Now nothing would ever matter again. I saw her turn the corner.

Up till that point I had almost managed to wipe Kurt from my mind. Even when Inga had occasionally referred to her brother, I'd felt nothing. It had been as if she was talking about a stranger, a German soldier that was one of the two who had died in a fire so long ago. My life with Inga had been my day to day reality. I was no longer connected to the past. I'd no longer expected this moment to arrive, ever. Now, after I had come to love Inga so desperately, suddenly I was thrown right back to the day when Kurt had died.

As soon as she had seen the headline, Inga had known that the body that had been dug up must be that of her brother. The location of the grave told her that. Her first impulse must have been to leave me immediately. She'd only stayed to ask me if maybe, maybe there could be the tiniest chance that I could tell her truthfully that I knew nothing about the body.

I went over it in my mind as I would a thousand times more, trying to think of what I could have done to avoid this catastrophic ending. Right at the beginning, when

State of Guilt

we met, I could have said that there had been a struggle and that it was a terrible accident. If I had told Inga the truth I would have betrayed Anja and, at the time, I could not have done that. Now it was too late. I knew that my Inga would never come back. I had lost her and with her everything that I valued in my life. I had lost my very existence. My worst fears had come true.

I had been fooling myself. I'd known all along, had expected, that sooner or later the truth would come out. If it had not happened, the expectation of Kurt's body being found would always have been with me and my whole life would have been a lie.

By protecting Anja, whom I had loved too much, I'd lost my own life. I saw those men chasing Kurt again, ready to kill him. Why didn't I tell them, 'Here he is'? What would have been the difference? The result would have been the same. Kurt would be dead. But could I have acted differently? I could never have let those men kill him any more than I could have killed him myself. If I'd handed him over to that murderous mob, I would've had to live with the knowledge that I'd been instrumental in his death.

It would have been better if I had agreed with Anja when she suggested that we leave the body in the alley behind the houses. I sat down at the table and let my tears flow.

CHAPTER TWENTY-EIGHT

After a sleepless night the doorbell rang early the next morning. 'She's back!' I called out, jumped out of bed, half put on my dressing gown and almost fell down the stairs in my haste to open the front door. It was Mum, plump, short and a little embarrassed. A hint of a smile passed across her face.

'Come in, Mum.' I stood aside to let her enter.

'I saw the newspaper and that story of the German body that was dug up in our street. It reminded me of that boy-soldier who came into our house. I thought I'd ask if you remembered him. We never really found out what happened to him, did we?' She was talking while we walked up the stairs.

'Yes. I've seen the story.' I followed her in and watched her sit down. I had no intention of answering her unspoken questions. How could I explain to her what had happened? Tell her that Anja had killed the soldier, that the story of the soldier dying in the fire was not true? I saw Anja's hard breasts again pushing against the thin dress, and the deadly determination in her eyes as she plunged the knife into Kurt and the look in his eyes, appealing to me, *'Hilfe –'*

'Inga not at home?'

'No, Mum. She's not. She's gone.'

'Gone where? I don't understand. Has she left you?'

I nodded.

'At the first sign of …'

'Look, Mum, I know you're concerned. I'm all right.' As I said that, I knew that it would take more than the rest of my life. I would never be "all right" again.

My mother's earnest blue eyes were questioning me, inviting me to tell her all my troubles, when all I wanted was to be left alone. There was no way that she, Dad, or anyone else could help me.

'I just thought … If there is a problem, maybe our minister might help. He would, I'm sure. He's so –'

'Can he change the past or bring back the dead? Look Mum, I'm not a little boy any more. Bible stories won't help me.'

'Well, I thought I'd see how you were,' she said again. 'I saw the paper and I thought maybe you'd need someone.'

Mum had tears in her eyes. She was hurt and I felt bad about that. I knew she must have taken the first train to arrive so early. I kissed her on both cheeks. 'For the moment I need to be by myself. I have to live my life in my own way.'

She walked to the door. 'Try to pray.' She was crying as she went down the stairs.

My anger evaporated. 'I'm sorry Mum.' I said and kissed her again before the door closed behind her.

I collapsed onto the sofa. I had been deliriously happy

with Inga. My first exhibition had opened. So what, who cares about those pictures now or about money or about anything. Had all this been inevitable? Now that the body was found, and Inga realised that it was her brother, the police would investigate, and it wouldn't take them long to come knocking at my door.

The phone rang. I ignored it. It kept ringing. At last I got up to answer it. It wasn't the police, it was Anja. 'Are you alone?'

'Yes.' Was all I could answer.

'Stay where you are. I'm coming over right now.' She hung up.

I did not want to see her. I hated her. Suddenly I was clear to me that it was Anja who had ruined my life. I'd never wanted to kill anyone. Anja had put me in this situation, while she herself had not been touched by the murder. How could I stop her coming to me? What did she want? Would she own up and tell the truth? If she would talk to Inga, then maybe …

Anja arrived all too soon. 'Lovely Piet, my poor lovely Piet.' She was brisk and bright-faced. 'You look as if you've been crying. You look terrible. I'll make you forget all about your silly worries,' she laughed. She followed me into the living room and stood in front of me. 'Actually, you don't look too devastated. Better than I expected.' She kissed my mouth, long and hard. I could feel her breasts against me. They were softer and seemed flatter than I remembered them.

My God. I did not want her, not now. Anja was Anja. If she felt like doing something, she would do it. I did not react at first, then felt my body responding and I hating myself for it. How could I. How could she? She

State of Guilt

was married with a family now. She had come to see me about Kurt. That was obvious. What did she want?

I had lost Inga, the woman I would always love. Yet in my misery my hands remembered and closed around Anja's buttocks as they used to. She had become slightly fleshier. I felt like crying again and I was clinging to her.

Softly I said her name 'Anja.' I wanted it to sound like a rebuke. Instead I pushed myself hard against her. Forget – I wanted to forget.

She smiled and held my head in her slim hands. 'Still the same Piet.' She looked deep into my eyes. I pushed her away as I felt a surge of sudden disgust.

She shrugged. 'We've got to talk, you and I. Have we got time before your Inga comes back?'

'She won't be coming back, not ever. Thanks to you, she won't.' I took the chair facing her and looked at her neck. I wanted to squeeze that lovely milk-white neck until her eyes popped out. Without her I would never be in this unbearable position.

Anja sat down, smoothing her skirt. 'What do you mean, thanks to me?'

She was unaware of the violent impulses I was prone to on seeing her sitting there so calmly. She felt in control. She looked around, 'Nice room. She has taste.' She indicated Inga's portrait. 'Is that her?'

Seething, I got up and took the portrait off the wall and laid it face down on the dresser. I did not want Anja even to look at Inga.

'Very good looking. Why won't she come back?' Then, as if she noticed me for the first time, 'Are you all right, my Piet? You look tense.'

My God, I thought. Anja is blind, stupid and blind. I

want to shake her to make her realise what she has done? I didn't want to tell her. I wanted to kill her. I could hardly speak. My throat was closed with searing hate. I stared at her. It took some long seconds before I could force myself to become calmer.

It gave me a sense of satisfaction to be brutal. 'Inga knows about Kurt.' I said bluntly.

Anja shook her head. 'That's impossible, don't talk nonsense. How could she? It's our secret. We agreed that neither you nor I would ever mention what happened that day to anyone. So nobody can prove anything, can they?' She frowned and I felt a small tingle of satisfaction.

I didn't want to explain to her about Kurt's papers. I didn't want her to know how it all happened. How I wanted to do the right thing and how Inga and I fell in love, and I didn't realise how much I loved her until it was too late. What would be the point. Anja would never understand.

'You didn't tell her about the soldier?' She shook her head in disbelief as I remained silent. 'You did, didn't you? No, Piet!' She screamed the last two words, and slumped back onto the sofa, her shoulders sagging and her hands at her sides like dead weights. 'Did you need to confess your sins? Did you tell her everything?'

I wanted to tell her, 'Yes, I told Inga that you killed the German and the police are on their way.' Instead I said, 'You needn't worry, Anja. I didn't tell her that it was you who killed Kurt. I promised you that nobody would ever know that.'

Anja looked relieved and let out a short laugh. 'Then … why should your Inga care about an old skeleton being dug up?'

State of Guilt

I said nothing for some moments. I couldn't think of a way to prepare her and didn't want to. 'Inga is Kurt's sister,' I said.

Anja's mouth fell open and closed again. The blood drained from her face. Unable to speak, she pointed at me, until she found her voice. 'How – how? You – Christ! That's – I don't believe it. You and she, she is – how is that possible?'

I nodded. It didn't matter any more, I didn't care any more. First Mum and now Anja. Why couldn't they all go away?

'Kurt had given me his papers and had asked me to send them to his family in case anything happened to him. So I sent them. Inga wrote back and we corresponded. She came over three years ago to find out where her brother had died.'

'Why ... this is sick!' She was screaming again, her face a mask of rage. 'Why didn't you burn his papers! What was the use of them? After all, he was the enemy! How could you be so stupid ... so utterly callous. Towards her, towards me, towards yourself even, your family.' She stopped mouthing words. 'She knew all along – that you were involved in killing her brother? God, and she still –'

I shook my head. Seeing her made me so weary, I closed my eyes, hoping that she would not be there when I opened them again. 'She didn't know. I didn't tell her what happened. She convinced herself that her brother was one of two Germans who were burnt to death in the empty house in Van Oldebarneveld Straat.'

'I remember it. You managed to make her believe

that? How utterly cruel and heartless. The poor woman!' She shook her head again.

'No, I didn't. I told you.' I felt my anger surging up again. 'Who are you to lecture me? Inga wrote to the police. They suggested that one of the two soldiers burned to death could have been Kurt. Inga made herself believe it and I let her. It was convenient. I couldn't tell her what had really happened, could I? It took the blame away from me, from us. After a while I got to believe it myself. What for Christ's sake are you complaining about, Anja? No one will ever suspect you.'

'It's sick. It's very sick, Piet.'

'Is it? I never wanted it to happen. I tried not to answer her letters, but she kept on digging, writing, wanting to know every detail. She was determined. In the end, out of desperation, to get rid of her, I gave her some addresses to write to, thinking they would be dead ends so that she would eventually give up, and that would be the end of it. Then she wanted to come and see where she believed her brother had died. When I met her, I fell in love, I wanted her, instantly. I knew she was the one I wanted to be with.'

Anja glared at me, her eyes wide. 'That's despicable. You don't know what love is! It's lust you felt. When you screwed her, you screwed everything. Why couldn't you have left things alone? You messed up her life and your own. It's weird, very weird, like something you might read in some fantastic novel, that never would or could happen in real life. Are you totally mad?'

I felt indifferent. 'Who are you to talk about love. I fell in love with Inga and I wanted to tell her everything, only I'd made my promise to you and suddenly it was too late. I wanted to be with her. I needed her desperately. That's all I could think of. Don't think it's been easy, living like that, never being able to relax completely, wondering if …'

'Phew! She must want to kill you right now.' She was calm now.

I only felt tired. 'You're right. I'm sure *you* would.'

She frowned, folding her arms She chose not to comment on my last remark. 'So what are you going to do now, Piet? Tell the truth? Confess for both of us? Are you going to screw up my life as well now? God! When everything could have been so simple. The soldier was just one more victim of the war and when his skeleton was dug up it would have taken a week for everyone to forget'

Anja didn't realise what I felt. My head was pounding with sudden hatred again. 'All I ever did was dig the grave. You're the one that stuck the knife into him.'

'You *would* say that. Your father wasn't killed by the Germans.' She spoke softly, almost a whisper.

I calmed down and felt bad about what I'd said. She was right. It was callous of me. I'd said it to excuse my own stupidity at posting Kurt's papers. 'I'm sorry. You'd better go.'

She sighed deeply and closed her eyes. I waited, not knowing or caring what to say or do.

When she opened her eyes they were shiny and very blue. She was calm, a different person from only minutes earlier. She leaned over and touched my cheek. 'My poor Piet. You carried all that guilt with you for all this time. I should've known. None of this would have happened to you if I hadn't come into your life. You would've done the right thing, looked after the soldier, given him your clothes and made sure that he got back safely to Germany, carried him there on your back if necessary and you would've felt that you'd been a good boy, and you would've been.'

You bitch, I thought.

'Well,' Anja smiled again. 'We all know what will happen next. You can bet that your Inga is very hurt and angry. She will probably go straight to the police, and they'll be wanting to talk to you pretty soon.'

She was right, I knew that, and I didn't care. I felt that I'd no control over the way things would turn out.

Anja was a quick thinker. She sat on my settee, back straight, long smooth legs crossed. 'What a mess you've got yourself into. You've created your own little circular hell, joining up your past, present and future. You can't be left to yourself. I should've married you after all, to keep an eye on you.'

It was getting dark and I got up and went over to the lamp next to the sofa.

'Don't put the light on, Piet. Come and sit next to me.'

'That's so like you, Anja. Make light of it. We're both guilty. It's not only my fault,' I said, spitting out a residue of anger, and sat at the opposite end of the sofa. 'I know that accessories to a crime are as guilty as the perpetrator, all the same – '

'I know, Piet, I know.' She didn't react to my anger. 'It isn't your fault at all. As you said, I'm the one who stabbed the German.' She stopped, 'But Piet, is there any need for both of us to confess?'

Her eyes where huge and seemed to attract the little daylight that was left and reflect it back at me, twice as bright. She spoke with a little tremor in her voice. 'It's not for me. I can cope with anything, you know that.

State of Guilt

I've got Maarten and the kids to think of. They don't know anything about what was between you and me, let alone about Kurt. The kids are still babies. If everything came out, it would destroy them. What we had was rather special. You remember that, don't you? That must count for something.'

I sat still and did not react.

Anja did not give me time to think further. 'I've always loved you, Piet.' She looked at me for some seconds and smiled, showing me that wonderfully reckless Anja that I remembered so well and, yes, had always admired. 'So nobody knows anything about my involvement with Kurt's death. I would like it to stay that way. Of course, if you really think there's a need, you can say it was me, … and … would anyone believe you?'

I almost felt like laughing as I thought; you know you'll get what you want. I considered arguing with her and denying her what she was asking from me, let the truth come out, and damn the consequences. She was right. It would make little difference to me, and I'd blame myself if Anja was arrested. I would let it happen, if for a moment I could believe that it would bring Inga back to me.

It was too late now, but there had been plenty of witnesses who'd seen that unruly and noisy bunch that chased Kurt and wanted to shoot him. We could have blamed them.

Dad might have wondered. He might have thought that it could be the same German that we'd held prisoner, no more than that.

Mum knew that I was involved, I was sure of that. I shook my head, smiling a wry smile. I knew too, that Anja was only thinking of Anja. Yet now that I had calmed down, I didn't hate her anymore. Somehow it was no longer important. Nothing would ever be important again.

'No Anja,' I said to her, 'it won't make any difference to me. There's no need for you to get involved. Go back to your nice life and leave me alone.'

She slid over to me, and let her skirt ride up. She took my hand and put it between her thighs. Though I didn't resist, I felt nothing. She touched my face and looked deep into my eyes as she began to undo the buttons of her silk blouse.

CHAPTER TWENTY-NINE

Inspector van Dalen had a smart office in which he sat behind a large, imposing oak desk. He was a big man with a well-proportioned square head and a straight nose. His close cropped greying hair looked prickly. The silver pen he held seemed too small for his hand. He looked at me calmly. The evenly tanned face made his light grey eyes look very pale.

He wore a well cut dark blue suit with a silk handkerchief in the top pocket of the jacket and looked more like a successful banker than a policeman.

'Why don't you give us the whole story,' he paused, 'right from the beginning, Mr. van Land.'

His voice was surprisingly soft and cultured and as he spoke his eyebrows, a shade darker than the hair, rose each time he emphasized a word. Highlights flashed behind his eyes. Just reflections, I thought, but I saw a kind of warning in them too. He showed no emotion as he spoke. Any frivolous remarks I might have been tempted to make, I suppressed.

I put two heaped spoons of sugar in the coffee in

front of me. I took a tentative sip and grimaced. It was lukewarm and horribly bitter.

'More sugar?'

I shook my head. No amount of sugar could save that coffee.

The inspector almost smiled. 'Tea perhaps?' His hand hovered over the cream-coloured phone.

I shook my head again. 'No, thank you.'

It was easy to relate the events leading up to Kurt's death. I told the inspector that we held Kurt prisoner in our house and of his subsequent escape on Liberation Day and how he turned up later that day chased by the mob and that I hid then him in our shed. Up to that moment, I could tell the truth, from then on adjustments had to be made. There had been ample time to work these out before the police came to see me. Anja had helped me make the story seem plausible. She had decided and I had agreed that we would not contact each other until we felt it was safe to do so.

I continued with my story. 'If I hadn't been there the German would've been killed by those men. Their leader was waving a pistol about, and if I hadn't hidden the soldier in our shed, the man would've shot him. He even pointed the pistol at me. I sent that mob the wrong way. I didn't want a defenceless man to be killed even if he was a German soldier.'

'A noble gesture,' van Dalen said, his voice completely neutral. 'Did you recognise any of the men?'

God, I thought. What is this man thinking, does he believe me? I looked away from him at the window which was almost totally filled with the dark branches of an oak tree, strong and powerful.

State of Guilt

When I turned back to face the inspector I had almost convinced myself that my story was true. I relaxed as I went on.

'No, I'd never seen any of them before or seen them since. I did wonder who they were. There were about six of them. When they'd gone, I waited for some time, maybe five minutes and went back into the shed to tell him that I would go and get him some of my clothes he could change into so that he would be safe, as long as he kept his mouth shut.'

I scratched my head slowly. It gave me time to formulate my words carefully. 'Either he hadn't understood my German or he panicked. He started to yell at me and push me. I pushed him back and told him to be quiet. He went berserk, screaming and spotted the small axe lying on the chopping block. He grabbed hold of it. I knew how sharp that axe was, as I'd sharpened it myself. It would slice through anything. So you can understand that I didn't want him near me with it. He started swinging it at me in a very threatening way. I didn't understand what he was screaming. I kept evading the axe and jumped out of the shed.'

Van Dalen nodded.

'I wasn't scared, he was no bigger than me. I felt calm. I was wearing my knife on my belt and I pulled it out, showed it to him and told him to stay back. I repeated that I would get him some of my clothes to change into. That's the first thing I wanted to do. *"Zivil Kleider, zivil Kleider!"* I kept saying to him. His eyes were crazed and he didn't listen to me. Maybe he was in a panic, as we had told him earlier that we would hand him to the Resistance.'

'Earlier?' Just one eyebrow raised this time.

'Yes, before Liberation Day, when he was our prisoner. We had to frighten him so he'd be quiet.'

'Oh, yes, you did say. Please continue,' the inspector picked up his coffee, looked at it and put it down again.

'Well, all at once he came straight at me with the axe. I stepped aside and called out to him to stop, but he swung at me again, all the while screaming in German. The axe was so close to my head that I could feel the rush of air. I had to stop him or he would've killed me, so I stabbed him. Never for a moment did I want to kill him. I had no choice.'

The inspector nodded. 'And then?'

My mouth was totally dry so I again tried a sip of the coffee. It now tasted even worse. I reached for the sugar and stirred a heaped spoonful into the awful liquid, tasted it and reached for the sugar again.

'The street parties were in full swing. That's where everybody was and that's where I wanted to be, where I'd been before that maniac confronted me. There was not a soul about in the alleyways at the back of the houses and nobody had seen him come into our garden. I hid his body in the shed under some empty sacks. I didn't know what to do. I didn't want to tell anyone. Who would have believed me? If that mob had found out I'd hidden a German, they'd have thought I was a traitor and want to kill me as well. I suppose I panicked.'

He nodded. 'I understand. Please continue,' he said again.

'As I said and I'm sure you know, the whole world was outside in the streets celebrating, so I joined them. After it became dark, I went back to our shed. The square was full of people so I trusted I would not be missed. I saw no

State of Guilt

one in the back lane, except a man and a woman in one of the gardens. They didn't hear me as they never stopped moaning as I went past. I started digging in the back yard of the bombed out house, number twenty-one. The soil was quite soft. It didn't take me long to dig a hole large enough to bury him in. He was heavy so I carried him, half dragged him there. I knew I had to do it, so I could. I let him slide into the hole and covered him up. I was only away from the party for about half an hour.'

'And you did this all by yourself? How old were you then?'

'I was fourteen. I can show you photographs of my class. I was the biggest and strong for my age. That soldier was smaller than me.'

'A skinny, starving fourteen year old boy who has hardly had anything to eat all winter? A likely story. Did your father help you, or your brother? Who are you trying to protect?'

'Nobody. It's true as I'm telling it to you. My family knew nothing about this. They were all at the party. My Dad won a prize. Ask him. Ask them all.'

'We will, Mr van Land, we will.'

'You'll find it's all true. I have always kept the whole thing to myself. It was too terrible to involve anyone. I knew it would devastate Mum and Dad and all the rest of my family. Everyone was so happy that day. How could I spoil all that? There was not going to be another day like it ever again. I did once try to tell Dad, but I couldn't go through with it. I thought it was better not to load the story on to him, because there was not much chance of the body ever being discovered.'

'Now you're going to tell me that you still have the

knife you used to kill Mr Grutz with, so that we have some evidence.'

'I lost that knife years ago on a camping holiday.'

The inspector sighed and rose. 'Miss Grutz came to see us, so the law will have to take its course. The remains will be formally identified from dental records, which are still available in Germany, Miss Grutz assures us. We will find out exactly what happened that day.'

As Inspector van Dalen was writing with his expensive pen, I looked at him intently and thought: Where were you in the war? Were you in the police then? I hope not because you might still have some Nazi sympathies and could easily have me arrested, or even worse, who knows? He looked hard enough to be prepared to do anything. No, a Nazi sympathiser would not have been made an inspector, would he? He probably has been an important figure in the Resistance or a war hero. Of course that might be equally bad if he wanted to show that Dutch justice was completely impartial.

He made some more notes and carefully placed the pen on the desk, then quietly looked at me again. 'Did *both* of you panic?'

'Both? No, you've got it wrong. I told you, I was alone – there was no one with me.' I had checked myself in time. 'You don't believe me, I can see that. But it happened as I told you, you will find. There was no one else involved.'

He did not answer, looked at me for a second or two and motioned me to the door. I felt sure that he would whip out a pair of handcuffs from under his desk, arrest me and have me conducted to a cell there and then. After all, I had just confessed to killing a man, even if it was self-defence.

State of Guilt

I was concerned and uncomfortable. Did Inspector van Dalen believe me, and if he didn't what would he do next? The room began to feel hot. These police cells wouldn't be as pleasant and casual as the army ones I'd been in. Even in the army I had imagined what it would be like to be in a real prison and I remembered the panic I had felt. If I were convicted of killing Kurt I could be in a cell for a long time. I pulled my shirt collar away from the sweaty skin of my neck.

'What will happen to me?' I asked. Damn it, my voice trembled a little.

'For the moment, nothing. Go home. We'll want to see you again tomorrow and then you will have to come in twice a week and sign on and please do not change your address without telling us.'

'Of course.' Relief flooded through me.

The inspector smiled, he was almost cordial. His voice sounded fatherly, and warm, but I was probably misreading him. It might be a ploy to make me relax and drop my guard. I would have to be careful with this man. He was experienced and would have little mercy. One mistake and the mess I was in would be even bigger. Then Anja and her children would be involved. I didn't want that to happen.

At last, exhausted, I was on my way to the station and home to Utrecht. I thought of phoning Anja from a public phone box and at once decided against it. The police might be following me. I had made enough mistakes. I knew that Anja was thinking of me, and that should have been a consolation. It was not. She probably was not even thinking about me.

It was early afternoon, when I got home. I had five

shots of jonge jenever and dropped on to the sofa. I fell asleep and slept until my stomach woke me and told me it was dinner time.

My head was aching and I swore when the doorbell rang. I decided to ignore it until a voice began to call through the letterbox. It was Albert. He had also moved to Utrecht and lived not far away from me now.

'Go away!' I called loudly and immediately regretted doing so as it was as if an anvil had been dropped on my head.

'Let me in, Piet. I want to talk to you.'

Albert had always been the extra wheel for me. Grown up and married now, he looked like a determined clerk with his little round glasses and that's exactly the job he had managed to get for himself and that was where he would stay.

'Okay, okay. Stop your noise.'

I struggled down the stairs and undid the latch.

'I brought you a bottle of lemon gin. Your favourite.'

'Don't like it any more.' I looked at him and felt sorry. None of this was his fault. I motioned for him to go on ahead. 'Come on up, Albert. We can drink it together.'

I followed him up and went into the kitchen to get a large glass of water. My head felt slightly better after I had drunk all of it.

Albert looked at the bottle on the small table in front of the sofa. 'You've had a few already?'

I ignored the question. 'Did Mum send you?'

'No, of course not. I wanted to see if you needed me. Inga gone?'

I nodded.

State of Guilt

'Pity, I liked her. And she loved you, so she might come back.'

I was reminded of our time during the war, when we used to go out together to get firewood from the forest, all those years ago, and decided he was a nice brother after all. 'Everything will be all right – I hope. No Albert, she won't come back. Here, have a gin.'

After I had poured for both of us we clinked glasses.

'Proost,' Albert said.

'And to you.'

'Piet, did you really have something to do with the body that was dug up in our old street?'

I told him briefly what I'd told Inspector van Dalen. Albert listened with wide open eyes.

Albert enjoyed talking about the war. Now it was in the past he liked to think of it as an exciting experience.

'God! What a thing to have done. I wish I had killed a Kraut.' He laughed. 'I'll never forget all those nasty Nazis. Remember that horrible fat man who confiscated our axe when we were caught cutting down a tree?'

'Yes, I remember. Albert, the war is over now.'

'I know that, but still … at least you did something about one of them.'

I took a sip of my gin, tilted the glass and emptied it. 'I don't want to talk about it, Albert. I think you should forget all that too. Killing is nothing to be proud of.'

'Come on, he was a German and one of them pushed Mum around, didn't he? Was it the same one? Don't you remember what Dad said? Those Germans would have killed us all if we had given them the chance.' He scrunched up his face as if in pain. 'Did the knife go in easily?'

'Shut up!'

'What a temper. I'm sorry I mentioned it.' He stood up, hurt at my outburst.

I sighed. 'Sorry. I don't want to be reminded.'

My little brother was only too ready to believe that I had killed the German. It had not entered his head that it might have been Anja's knife sliding into Kurt. That was good, as everyone else would probably think the same. Inspector van Dalen might have doubts that I killed the German and buried him all by myself yet he could not be sure.

'Come, I'll buy you a rijsttafel at the Indonesian.'

'Thanks.' Albert's face relaxed into a grin. 'In case you needed me, I have already asked Carla not to wait for me with dinner, and I'm starving.'

CHAPTER THIRTY

As we were putting on our coats the doorbell went again.

'Go and see who that is, Albert, and tell them I am not in.'

'It might be Dad.'

'Still say I'm not in. I've already talked to Mum.'

While I went to have a last pee Albert went down, shaking his head. I heard the murmur of voices, and after a minute or two he came back up. 'It's reporters from *Het Klaroen*. They want to talk to you.'

'What the hell for? The police must have told them my name. Tell them to go away. We want to eat.'

Albert went down and came straight up again. He sounded excited. 'They won't go away. They ask for only one minute. Come on, Piet. That can't hurt. Some more reporters have arrived. They are all waiting at the front door.'

What could they want with me? What could I possibly tell them? That I wanted to die? I sighed and flopped down on the sofa. 'Let's get it over with.'

All at once the living room was full of them, some carrying cameras. Without asking if I minded, flash bulbs exploded in my face. I was grateful that Albert was there. He answered most of the questions that were fired at me from all directions. I didn't communicate beyond a nod or a head shake.

Albert was in his element. 'Yes, Piet is a photographer. If you want to see his best pictures you should go to the *Gallerie Fotografiek*.'

I wished he would shut up. It seemed to go on and on, until at last they had what they wanted and left.

'You'll be in the papers tomorrow,' Albert said.

'Come on,' I said. 'Let's go quickly before more of them turn up.'

* * *

The rijsttafel was tasteless; I could only eat half of it.

'You can come with me to the gallery,' I said to Albert after I had paid the bill.

'It's closed now, isn't it?'

'Wim Jansen, the owner, lives above it so that's no problem. I want to get some pictures out of there.'

I felt that the pictures I had taken of Inga as the girlfriend of a German soldier should no longer be exhibited. I could not stand the thought of seeing her face at the gallery and be reminded of her hair gradually growing back as it was shown in each succeeding photo. Besides, it seemed wrong to continue to exhibit the work that she'd been such an all-important part of. Without Inga … My misery increased again. I could not live with those pictures around me.

It took a little while to get Wim to answer his doorbell.

'I've had three calls from newspapers about you,' he said.

'So?' I was not pleased.

'It's all right, Piet. It's great. You'll get publicity now.'

'I might be in prison, too. It won't be much good then, will it?'

Wim shrugged. 'Have you come to tell me that?'

'No, to collect the "Girl Series".'

'What! Why?'

I explained my feelings about the portraits to him. While Wim argued that they were important, I kept insisting until at last he threw up his hands and gave in.

After we had collected the pictures and were nearing home, I asked Albert to go ahead and look for activity near my front door. All was quiet on the windswept street, not a reporter in sight. It was getting late. As we went inside, Albert kept chatting. I learned that he never needs an alarm clock to wake up and that Carla hated him wearing brown shoes, which he liked. Listening to Albert droning on was relaxing. At last he stopped talking and went home.

I wrapped the pictures we had picked up from the gallery in brown paper, and stacked them in the small space I had above the ceiling under the roof. Out of sight. Something else to forget, I thought.

* * *

The next day was confusion and bedlam. I gave up trying to work and cancelled what appointments I had for the next few days. Everyone wanted to speak to me. The newspapers, radio and television.

Suddenly, to my consternation, I was a hero. The

papers dubbed me *Boy-Hero*. The murder that I had so desperately wanted to prevent, was billed as my victory. "BOY HERO KILLS EVIL NAZI", was a typical headline. It was ironic and I hated it. Nobody waited for the police or the courts to decide whether my story was true or who the German was. They did not wait to find out who Kurt was, whether he was even a Nazi.

I fled to Franeker, the little city where I had spent the first nine years of my life, where I had been a child in the true sense of the word. I walked along the narrow, red-brick-paved streets, flanked on each side by small seventeenth century houses, and along the still canals with their winter-bare trees. I began to recover.

The house we had lived in was still there and I stood looking at it for some moments, until the net curtains moved. Turning left and into Vossegatsteeg I was eight years old again, dying for a piss, not wanting to go home, as Klaas, my friend was waiting. The street was deserted, so I stood at the edge of the canal and directed my steaming stream at the flowers of the just formed ice, making lovely circles, wondering how much of the ice I could melt.

Without warning a tremendous force hit my head. It reverberated inside my skull. As I turned, there was Mum. Before she allowed me to go outside, she had seen, as I was crossing my legs, that I should first have gone to the toilet, and she'd followed me, wondering if, when and where I would relieve myself.

The memory made me smile and I decided that I was ready to go back to Utrecht. I was a day late signing on at the police station the sergeant informed me. I said I was sorry and he said no more.

The newspapers speculated, as I did, on my future.

State of Guilt

The general consensus was that I must not be sentenced to a term in prison. I felt relieved by that. One even said that I should get a medal.

I went to the gallery on my return, and saw a small crowd peering at my pictures. A sprinkling of red dots had appeared beside my photographs.

'Where the hell have you been?' Wim spotted me at once. 'Look. Come and look.'

The rise and fall of voices followed me into his small office. He pointed to the open book. 'You've sold prints of most of your images.'

I was stunned. 'It must be your framing.'

'You're good. They're great images, all of them, and now that you're famous, everybody wants them. Some of the buyers took more than one. Incredible. Do your bit, get out there and talk to people. I'll bring out some wine. There's plenty left over from the opening.'

Dutifully I did as told and I spent the next hour explaining my landscapes and avoiding questions about Kurt. It did cross my mind that ninety-five out of a hundred of these people only set foot in the *Gallerie Fotografiek* because they believed that I had killed a German. It felt unreal, as if it were happening to someone else. I was grateful for the success; it was what I had dreamed of, but at what cost? The greatest success could never compensate me for losing Inga.

Finally the crowd thinned and Wim appeared at my side. 'Happy?'

'I'm surprised.'

'You don't look or sound very excited.'

'It is the way it's happening, Wim. I have lost the one woman I will ever love. People only come out of their interest in lurid sensationalism. If you remember, hardly anyone came to the opening.'

'Never mind that. This is the new you, Piet.' He threw out his arms, and made a half turn, indicating the exhibition. 'Come, I'll get you a list of the prints you will need to do. Over twenty so far.'

'Can we wait a few days?'

'Not a good idea, Piet. We still have to do the framing and clients like to take possession of their acquisitions as quickly as possible.'

As I would have to answer charges about Kurt's death, it made sense to start on the prints while I was still certain of my freedom. The concentration needed to produce the prints would distract me and force me not to become morbidly obsessed with the trial. 'I'll start tomorrow.'

CHAPTER THIRTY-ONE

On a wet Friday morning, Mum, Dad, and Albert and Carla waited with me for some considerable time in one of the reception areas of the Amsterdam District Court. Finally my lawyer, Hubert Veilinga appeared. We shook hands and he sat with me. He was in a buoyant mood, reassuring me and complimenting me on the way I was dressed. As instructed by him I wore a dark blue suit, white shirt with cuff links and a specially bought tie, not too loud, not too wide. 'Good. You look entirely presentable and civilised.'

I entered the court room with Hubert. Dark wood panelling all around the walls, parquet floor, and all the furniture, benches, chairs, lawyers' tables, judges' table and high-backed chairs, everything made of dark solid oak. Eight yellow glass globes, spaced a few metres apart, hung suspended from the plaster roses on the high ceiling. The lights did little to brighten up the large room although the ceiling was white and continued almost half a metre down to where it met the panelling.

Veilinga motioned me to sit down at one of three

tables, next to him and his pile of papers. He had already told me, 'We will play the self-defence card. The publicity that your case has had will help. The media are describing you as a hero. Of course the judge must not allow himself to be influenced by public opinion. He was active in the Resistance during the war; that may help our case. Again, that should not be a factor. Nevertheless he is human. It's better to have him on the bench than a former Nazi.'

Hubert rubbed his hands together, folded them across his chest, and took a deep breath. 'Then again, he may feel that justice should be done and that he needs to be severe.'

I sighed, 'Are you sure you've covered every eventuality?' I asked as I sat down.

'Trust me, Piet. You will be a free man by the end of my performance.'

'Are you a good actor, Mr Veilinga?'

He smiled, even more broadly this time. 'I am, Piet. I am.'

* * *

Mum and Dad were sitting in the public gallery with Albert and Carla, who was probably thinking that she had always known I was no good. I had not expected her to come and wondered about her motives for being present. Curiosity? Schadenfreude?

Anja and Rose, Anja's mother, were there too, and I noticed Wim Jansen, the owner of the Gallery, no doubt already calculating how the proceedings would affect the sales of my photographs. There were some acquaintances and an attendant.

I could not see Inga. I hoped that she had signed a statement and would not need to attend.

State of Guilt

'All rise,' the attendant called out.

The judges came in, all three dressed in long black robes with a white bib.

'Good morning. Please be seated,' said the president who sat down in the chair in the middle on the slightly raised platform. He was flanked by the two other judges: one a matronly woman, mousy-haired, wearing outsize spectacles. The only make-up she wore was a hint of rouge on her cheeks. The other judge was a dark haired man of around fifty with a clipped moustache on a small face devoid of all expression.

Judge Nicolas van Vecht, the president, was lean, had a pink face and a good head of healthy white hair. He wore gold-rimmed spectacles and his voice was almost friendly. I decided not to let his soft voice raise any hopes.

Inspector van Dalen's voice had not been loud either yet he had seemed hard and tough to me. He had been very persistent before drawing up his official report and he had thought it worthwhile to forward it to the public prosecutor, who in turn must have felt that he had a reasonable chance to get me convicted of the charges against me. The thought made me sweat, and I again remembered my army cell, cold and damp.

On the judges' right sat the prosecutor and on their left the clerk of the court.

First of all the judge asked my name and address and when he was satisfied that I was who he thought I was, he asked the prosecutor to please proceed.

The prosecutor, whose name was Dorsten, was tall and thin. He wore a black gown and looked as serious as a Calvinist minister and could double as the Angel of

Death. His hollow-cheeked head, pivoted on an unusually long neck.

He managed to get my attention as he began his address to the presiding judge. As I had expected, Mr Dorsten had a monotonous, booming voice. It went with his bleak countenance. He cleared his throat and began:

The accused is charged with the following:

1.

that he, the accused, on or about 5 May 1945 in the town of Hilversum, with intent, took the life of Kurt Grutz, and that the accused with that intent struck the aforementioned Kurt Grutz several times, at any rate at least once (with strength) with (a) knife (knives) in the (upper) body, as a result of which the aforementioned Kurt Grutz passed away.

2.

that he, the accused, hereinbefore mentioned on or about 5 May 1945 in the town of Hilversum, when he had taken the life of Kurt Grutz, the accused then with intent did proceed to dig a grave approximately seventy centimetres deep and two metres long by fifty centimetres wide.

He then took the lifeless body of the victim of his crime and unlawfully buried the aforementioned body in the grave he had dug with the intent of concealing the body of the aforementioned Kurt Grutz.

I had the impulse to smirk at this legal language. It seemed to me that as both the police and the public prosecutor had my statements with my confession, the whole procedure could have been simplified by handing the papers to the judge beforehand. Then all he had to do was pronounce judgment. If I was to spend time in a cell, I'd rather start it quickly without having to sweat over it for weeks.

Dorsten continued, 'Who are we dealing with? Mr. van Land is the kind of person who kills a man and afterwards seduces the victim's sister.'

I found that particular statement very painful. The only blessing was that Inga was not present.

Then Dorsten read out a sworn statement from a Münster dentist, who positively identified teeth and molars as belonging to his patient known as Kurt Grutz. 'The prosecution thanks you Mr. President.'

Dorsten sat down and the president repeated the charges of which I stood accused and asked me if I understood.

As I answered, 'Yes,' he asked the other two judges, who had only moved occasionally to scratch their heads or rub their chins, whether they had anything to add. Not unexpectedly they did not.

The Chairman then said, 'Could we now hear from Master of Laws Veilinga who is representing Mr. van Land.'

Master Veilinga touched my arm and stood up.

'No one asked the Germans to bomb Rotterdam and no one asked them to invade Holland. No one asked them to force their way into our houses and no one asked that particular soldier, who we now know as Kurt Grutz, to try and steal food from an already starving family.'

Veilinga paused for some seconds and glanced around the courtroom. I winced as I thought of Inga and I wished I could put my arms around her and feel her arms around me. 'Don't say these things,' I thought.

Johannes Kerkhoven

I knew Veilinga was defending me, but I wanted to call out to him. 'I don't care what happens to me.'

Hubert was not finished. 'That soldier of the German Reich pushed Mrs van Land to the floor.'

'He did.' Mum called out loudly from the public gallery at the back of the room.

I turned and could see Dad nudge her and pull at her coat to make her sit down.

'There will be no interruptions from the public,' the President said.

'He did push me to the floor,' Mum said, softer this time.

'Madam! Please continue Counsel, if you would be so good as to stick to relevant facts.'

'Your Honour. I merely want to show what kind of person forced his way into the van Land household. The children came to Mrs van Land's aid when she was attacked and in their panic held the soldier prisoner, a not inconsiderable feat, and a very dangerous one. If this had been discovered by the Germans or if the family had been betrayed by a Nazi sympathiser, recriminations from the Germans would have been instant and deadly.

After being held prisoner for one night, the enemy soldier escaped and instead of rejoining his unit, he returned to Mr. van Land's family for help. Mr Grutz, still dressed as a German soldier, had obviously panicked when the Liberation came that very same day. My client, being humane and not vengeful, saved the soldier from a group of men chasing him and was prepared to lend the German some of his own civilian clothes. The German however attacked my client, then only fifteen years old, with an axe and would have killed him if my client had not defended himself.'

State of Guilt

Exclamations of incredulity and surprise came from the public gallery.

Veilinga's thin lips widened very slightly giving his hook-nosed face a hint of satisfaction. 'Mr President, the evidence clearly explains that my client had no choice in this matter. He did not ask this German soldier to attack him, when the soldier did so, the boy, because please remember that he was only a boy, could have panicked so easily, he did not. Instead, he still wanted to help the German. This offer of help was not only rejected, but the soldier proceeded to attack the boy. That boy, who sadly had to grow up with this terrible secret and who is now before you as my client, stands here as a hard-working, honourable man. Therefore, Mr. President, therefore I plead that my client acted in self-defence against an enemy soldier. Indeed he merely exercised his right to defend his own life. Therefore if it so pleases the court, we ask for understanding and leniency for that boy and dismiss the charges that are brought against my client.'

God, I thought. This man is brilliant. I could listen to him all day and I was beginning to believe his words. Perhaps I am brave after all.

'The prosecution, Mr. President,' Veilinga continued, 'attempted to blacken my client's character for having a relationship with the soldier's sister. However, Mr. President, when my client found the dead soldier's papers, he could have burnt them. He did not. His sense of right and wrong made him return these papers to the soldier's family in Germany, thinking that that would be the end of it. The soldier's sister, however, having come to believe that her brother had died in a house fire, insisted on coming to Holland to see where her brother had supposedly died. When she met my client, she fell passionately in love with him. My client responded and so out of death, came love. The defence thanks the court.' He sat down.

'It was not like that!' I wanted to call out. I felt Veilinga's hand on my shoulder as I half rose to stand.

The presiding judge said, 'Has the accused anything to say?'

I got up, and rattled off what I'd rehearsed. 'Everything I have to say Sir, is in my statement. I have nothing to add to that. I hope the Court will understand the inevitability of the events that were thrust upon me.'

Judge van Vecht nodded at me in a friendly way and said, looking around the room, 'Very well. This court is now in recess and will reconvene in two weeks' time, when we will give our judgment on both charges.'

* * *

Despite the events of the day I slept very well. Mum and Dad invited me to stay with them for the weekend and so did Albert and Carla. I think Carla even meant it. When I declined their offers, Dad suggested we all go for a meal so I knew my family was on my side.

I was touched by their loyalty even though I would have preferred to go straight home. The meal was uneventful. It seemed to me that the more my family displayed their emotions, the better I could master mine. So the meal had its uses.

The weekend was a non-weekend, marked by so many phone calls that I fled my home and slept in a hotel on Saturday night.

* * *

Two weeks later I again dressed with care on Veilinga's suggestion. Same blue suit, white shirt and quiet tie.

State of Guilt

The judge wasted little time. On the first charge, he read out that 'He the accused – ', then the whole bit again complete with 'aforementioneds', until he came to 'Kurt Grutz passed away'. The Court found that I was not guilty as we had successfully pleaded self-defence.

Tears of relief welled up behind my eyes. I had not realised how much the proceedings had affecting me. I struggled to stop myself from sobbing loudly.

My eyes were closed and I was only vaguely aware of the murmur of voices as everyone in the courtroom reacted. I didn't hear Judge van Vecht as he continued with the second charge of unlawful burial until he said the word 'guilty'. I looked at him then and at Veilinga, who put his arm around my shoulder. 'Don't worry,' he whispered.

The Judge in his calm voice continued and I realised that the sentence of nine months detention he had mentioned seconds before was suspended and conditional.

Veilinga pulled me to him and hugged me. 'What did I tell you? You're free to go, Piet.'

CHAPTER THIRTY-TWO

Sudden success is a powerful medicine. After initial feelings of embarrassment, I began to feel comfortable in the personality of the famous boy hero. It's good for the ego to read about oneself in glowing terms, and to receive many letters of congratulation. I did get a few hate letters, which I ignored. They were obviously from Nazi sympathisers or cranks.

The media decided that their tremendous efforts had helped in getting me discharged. Now they wanted their exclusives. They pursued me for weeks on end, even followed me to Terschelling where I'd rented a small cottage, to get some peace. Not one of the newspaper reports expressed any horror at the killing.

Wim Jansen was ecstatic. All he cared about was the fact that the timing of the trial could not have been better for my exhibition. From being an unknown, one of many photographers with the prospect of selling a few prints, I was selling prints by the dozen.

I was successful and respected. Probably envied by many. What did not show was the pain I still felt. Inga

State of Guilt

might have physically gone out of my life but she was always on my mind, even during busy days. I still hoped for the impossible, to have a chance to see her again, to talk to her, to love her. Then depression would strike and in my misery and anger I would shift the blame to Anja for what she had done.

I also felt that I was betraying myself. Had my love for Inga been superficial after all? I had been so certain that it would last forever. I took down Inga's portrait from my living room wall. It was too painful to see her smiling down at me. After a time it became difficult for me to bring her image clearly into my conscious mind. The impossible was happening, my memory of her was fading.

Time can not be stopped or reversed and keeps doing what it does best: putting distance between the past and the present, unaware of whether we see it as a blessing or a curse. I could not change history. Would I even want to? If the truth were to come out I would no longer be seen as a hero.

I became more absorbed in my work. I liked the new me. I was admired, an artist and I was someone who had done what most of the population of an occupied country would have liked to do: I had killed one of the oppressors. How many times had I told the story now?

By retelling it over and over again, I had almost convinced myself that it was the true version of events. The more I adopted the persona of hero, the more the memory of Inga receded into the past.

At any rate, there were no choices to be made. I was trapped. If I decided to tell the truth, it would be like committing suicide. I would be annihilated and be exposed as a fake, a coward, a nobody who had cheated. I would not be able to look anyone in the eye. Considering the consequences, I was not about to exchange a successful, pleasurable life for a non life. Anja knew how I felt and she was happy for me. My secret was safe with her as hers was with me.

There were post Inga relationships, all superficial. Anja was also there. When we'd made love the day Inga left it had, for me, been a betrayal. I had not wanted to, I was mourning, yet Anja had given me comfort. Paul was right when he wrote in the Bible: The mind is willing but the flesh is weak. After the flesh had given in, I felt angry with myself and with Anja, a feeling that did not persist for very long. We stayed in regular, if sporadic, contact.

One day, about six months after Inga had left, Anja called. 'I have to see you, Piet, today.'

I protested, 'I'm about to go out on an assignment.' It was true, I was literally loading my equipment into the car. 'I really can't postpone this. Too many people are relying on me. Tomorrow, any time.'

We met for lunch the next day in a café where we had met before, badly lit and in a side street. She was wearing a skirt and silk blouse, with the two top buttons undone. She sat down and leant over the small table. She was not wearing a bra and with a tingling feeling I remembered how perfectly those breasts had always fitted in my hands.

She knew I was looking and smiled sweetly, cupping the wine glass in both hands and taking her time to sit up straight. 'So, here we are, you and I. Of course I knew you'd find the time.' She put her glass down and picked up the menu. 'I'm starving.'

State of Guilt

An hour later we were having coffee and still Anja had not mentioned why she wanted to see me so urgently.

'Well? You seem very relaxed. What was so urgent, Anja. There are still a few things I want to do this afternoon.'

'Mm, I do feel relaxed, Piet. It's being with you, and this coffee is good too, don't you think?' She took a sip.

'As always.'

'I've left Maarten.'

I sat up. 'You what!? No. I don't believe you.'

'Yes, I have.' Her head tilted sideways.

'I'm really sorry. I feel it's my fault.'

'Not at all,' Anja laughed. 'You're flattering yourself. The fact is that Maarten and I were never really equally matched. It was a mistake. His mistake. He felt he needed to master me, like an old-fashioned domineering husband. If Maarten said "jump", he expected me to do so. He could not understand that I'm not his property. He didn't realise that when he felt he *had* mastered me, it was only because I was pretending to submit to him, for the sake of peace. If I did not feel like doing that, he would sulk for days until I made the first move. These arguments always look silly after a few days, arguments about nothing. Then, without warning, Maarten began to get physical when an injury to his male pride became too much for him.'

'He hit you?' I could not imagine the quiet schoolmaster raising anything other than his voice, and then only slightly.

'Yes, he did.' The skin on her face tightened. 'He was on his knees afterwards, and begged me to forgive him. I didn't let him see my fury and said that I did forgive him. I had to consider my children, even before myself.'

'It was only the once then?'

'No, it was not. When he hit me the second time I knew that there was going to be a pattern and that I would have to get away from him. If he hit me a third time I would lose my temper and defend myself. I didn't want that to happen. How would my kids survive?' Her lips pressed together and her eyes hardened. It was the look I had seen on her lovely face once before.

I wondered what her kitchen looked like and imagined the knives. 'I had no idea. He seemed such a mild fellow.' I suddenly felt cold and shivered.

'Well, now you know. Maarten has a vicious temper. If he stayed calm he would win most arguments. He's quite a brilliant man.' She relaxed and smiled again. 'My poor Piet, I feel a little guilty about loading this onto you. As if you haven't done enough for me already.'

'Don't mention it.'

She had come to me again because she was having problems and on the one hand I was pleased about that, it made me feel wanted, on the other I could see clearly that Anja was going to ask me to do something or other. Yet I was pleased that she was no longer with Maarten. No one not even Anja could ever replace Inga, but Anja was so much part of my life and I of hers, that it seemed natural that we would share each other's troubles. When I made a half-hearted effort to try and get her to talk to someone, maybe patch up her marriage, she was adamant that if she returned to Maarten it would end in tragedy.

'He has no idea of what might happen and I am not going to let him find out.'

'What will you do? What about the children?'

'They will stay with Maarten for the moment. That's

how he wants it. His widowed mother, who I never got on with, could not wait to move in with him. For the time being I will stay with Mum.' She cleared her throat, 'Unless you have space in your bed?' She touched my hand. 'I don't mind if you don't. Is there someone sharing your life at the moment?'

I smiled. This was Anja. So that's why we're sitting here. We have had our lunch. Then, pow! she springs her news on me. She was not even in a hurry, she knew that good old Piet would always be there. She assumed that I would be happy to welcome her back into my bed. One day she is married to Maarten and miles away, almost completely out of my life, the next she assumes we are a couple, as if she had never been out of my life, and in a sense that was true.

'Phhht! Anja, you're going too fast for me. I do love you and I love being with you. You know that. Can you give me a few days to think it through?'

She smiled happily. 'Of course, my Piet. As long as you like.'

I had been thinking about buying a house for some time and had viewed a property on the outskirts of Utrecht. It had a large garage, with a pitched, tiled roof, stepped down from the main house, with enough height and space inside for it to accommodate my studio and darkroom. The land in front of the house sloped gently to the road. It was mostly lawn, edged by shrubs and flowerbeds.

The dark green front door gave access to the wide, not very long hallway. One door, on the left, opened to a cloak room, next to that was the staircase to the first floor, while the door straight ahead from the front door gave access to a spacious living room, with French doors leading into the garden.

The house was surrounded by large oak trees, and I had fallen in love with it. The day after my talk with Anja, I went back for a second look. Driving up to the house I imagined living there with Anja. I decided that if she hated it, I would still buy it and we would not live together.

I had finally reached a stage in life where I knew what I wanted. I'd survived without Anja for enough years now. I still loved her, I always would, but I told myself firmly that I wasn't the same man she had walked out on years ago.

CHAPTER THIRTY-THREE

'I agree with everyone.' Anja said. 'You are a hero. What you did for me took real courage. Most boys of the age you were when the German died would have run away and left me to cope by myself. Life is compensating you for what you did for me, and not before time.'

'Now you are flattering me and I like it. I might take advantage of you.' I put my arms around her.

She grabbed me by the ears and pulled my face down onto hers and her cool tongue darted into my mouth.

* * *

I no longer needed to try and market my work. There were approaches by publishers who wanted to put my photographs into glossy coffee table books. I was asked to lecture on photography to rooms full of eager young faces, and lapped up their admiration. There were more exhibitions, national and international, and each time, the same old story was dragged out again by the newspapers. After eight years I was still the teenage hero. It sold photographs and books, lots of them. I fitted perfectly into the personality of the person who, the whole world was telling me, was Piet van Land. There was money and that made me feel good

It was as if the years were stored in glass boxes in my memory. The glass box, where Inga lived, gradually became more and more opaque with the dust of time. Despite my success, it made me feel at times that I was betraying my innermost feelings because, while I had been convinced that Inga was essential to my happiness, the anguish of losing her was no longer part of me. I was forgetting her.

The nightmares that still managed to escape from the Kurt-box in my memory were losing their power. I'd learned to cope with them. In the dream he would always come at me with the axe, gradually however, his movements became slower. I had read that in anxiety dreams it helps if you confront the danger that faces you, whatever it is. In later dreams I was able to take the axe away from him. The nightmares became less frequent until they ceased altogether. I had mastered them. The Kurt-box was closed.

Luckily there was that other glass box in my head with all the memories of Anja in it. The lid on that one stayed open so that all of my memories concerning her were accessible and the past and the bright present could merge.

During moments when the memories of Inga became irresistibly strong, I could shrug them off and look at them as simply tricks of the mind. I knew that Inga was no longer with me and that Anja was. I had become perfectly satisfied with that.

Anja and I never married but would always be lovers.

State of Guilt

I did broach the subject of marriage once. Anja felt that that would be too much of a good thing. It would ruin the feelings she had for me, she said. Occasionally I felt a longing for the children I could have had. I imagined what it would be like to have a son or a daughter. I never told Anja about this because I had only ever wanted children with Inga. That would never happen now and I kept these thoughts to myself. So life went on year after year.

I saw Dad and Mum infrequently and they never mentioned Inga. I knew they had tried to like Inga. After she had gone it was as if they had never met her. There's a good Calvinistic axiom: Anything that might be unpleasant or in any way disturbing must be firmly ignored. Very workable. Even Albert lost interest in me eventually. His work was very important work to him. Besides he had Carla and the three children to support, and on his clerk's salary that must have been a challenge.

I wondered how much Carla bullied him. It was as if she had two faces. She was still young, nice looking. I seldom saw her smile. Her blue-grey eyes would darken dangerously as they looked at me from under her wrinkled brow. I imagined how she would look at seventy. Her lips thinner and her nose and chin longer.

CHAPTER THIRTY-FOUR

I was having breakfast and could see the postman coming up the driveway. I finished my coffee and scooped up the letters. Among the bills, there it was, without the slightest warning, sent on from my old address. The clear rounded handwriting, even after all this time, told me instantly that it was from Inga.

It was as if a sledgehammer shattered the two glass memory boxes in my mind, where I had filed away all my memories of Kurt and above all of Inga. Shards of memory flew everywhere, voices, laughter, visions of love and terror, leaving my mind raw and throbbing, filling it to bursting point with vivid memories, suddenly revived. I had been lulled into complacency by the passing years, they were there all the time, waiting patiently, silently, like a seed lying dormant during droughts and then when the rain comes, bursts into life, grows and blossoms. So my memories had lain there until they were ready to torment me again. Time was no longer linear, it condensed and the past became the present.

Sweat appeared on my forehead as I saw Kurt's dead,

headless body burst into the room, again blindly swinging his blood-stained axe at me. I could hear and feel the swish-swish again as the axe cut its terrifying slicing path through the air, ever closer to my face. And I could see Inga's eyes looking at me, indescribably sad, as she walked out of my life.

Holding the letter in my hand I turned it over. The handwriting, the stamps. I turned it over again and was reminded of my hesitation when I received her first letter. If I had not opened that very first one ... Would it be better if I burnt this one right now, without opening it?

I knew I would open it. How could I bear not to know what she said?

I shook my head. This is ridiculous. It's so long ago now, and I've had enough. My fingers trembled as I ripped the side of the envelope. I unfolded the single sheet of paper.

Dear Piet,
It is with difficulty that I write to you, and I am sorry to be so blunt. Kurt, my son, has insisted that I send this letter. Kurt wishes to come to Holland to see you, as you are his father.

I stopped reading, I was stunned. I have a son! A son. But how? Inga must have been pregnant when she had left all those years ago! She had never let me know. My son must be almost a man by now, around fifteen years old I quickly calculated. A wave of confusion mixed with bitter regret flooded my consciousness.

Would it be convenient for you if he came to

visit you? We would understand if you had rather he did not come after all this time.

I am sorry this letter is so brief and I don't know if we are doing the right thing. However, Kurt is not to be dissuaded from his intention to meet you.

Yours sincerely,
Inga

A son whom I'd never seen and he was coming! Whom I had never seen as a baby, or a little boy, growing up into a young man going to school, and a son who had never seen me.

Questions flashed through my mind. Had Inga told him how his uncle had died? What will he think of me, and why has she only now written about his existence? Has Inga told him everything? She might have reverted to the story that I had allowed her to believe initially, that his uncle had died in a fire. Perhaps he knows nothing about me. That must be it. I felt another rush of joy as I read the letter again; a son. Would he look like me?

What does it matter, I have a son. I had to tell someone. Anja. She would be home soon. I would tell her. She would be happy for me. I only saw Mum and Dad and Albert and Carla at weddings and funerals now. I imagined their faces, serious and unbelieving, shaking their heads. I could feel them thinking about my news already, as if they were saying, 'This boy is just appearing out of nowhere. How do you know he is yours?'

They had liked Inga, I knew that at the time, although she had never been fully accepted, despite her efforts. She had always welcomed everyone warmly when they visited us on rare occasions. She had wanted to be part

State of Guilt

of my family. Eventually Inga, generous as she was, could no longer cope with the surly, wooden reactions of my relatives. She had never given up, equally she had never made any progress apart from a grudging smile now and then. Albert was the exception. He and I would always be close and he had loved Inga.

* * *

When I told Anja the news and showed her the letter, she did not respond immediately. 'That's wonderful,' she said. Her voice sounded flat. 'I'm happy for you.'
Her muted reaction only registered on a secondary level and did nothing to dampen my enthusiasm. 'I can't wait to see him. Will he look like me? What sort of a person will he be?'

Thousands of questions raced through my mind and I talked non-stop about the son I had never met. The things I wanted to tell him and show him. What Kurt and I could do together. Not much work was done that day.

That night I did not even want to think about making love, I was still too excited to think about anything other than my son.

When I leant over to give her a final goodnight kiss, her face was wet. 'You're crying.'

'Yes, I … I'm happy for you. I don't think I've ever seen you more excited than you are right now. It's wonderful to see, but I'm a little sad for you too and concerned. Why now? What does this boy know about you?'

'Inga obviously hasn't told him about what happened to her brother, otherwise why would he want to come and see me?'

'You've never forgotten Inga, have you?'

'I ... you were my first love,' I kissed her ear. 'And my last one,' I added and I meant it.

Was Anja sad about her children or was she uneasy about Kurt coming? Kurt. It was disconcerting that my son was called Kurt. He would be a living reminder of the German Anja and I had buried.

'I don't like the name she's given him, but I understand why she did it,' I felt my heart begin to race, 'What if he looks like his uncle?'

Anja tightened her arms around me. 'Don't look too far ahead Piet, in any case, we are together and together we will always cope.'

CHAPTER THIRTY-FIVE

Answering Inga's letter was difficult. The guilt and pain came back in force, alternating with joy in the knowledge that I had a son. There was so much I wanted to ask and tell Inga. I wanted to bridge the years of our separation, but thought I did not have the right to step back into her life unless she invited me. I left the letter as short as her own had been.

> Dear Inga,
> To know that I have a son makes me very happy and at the same time sad, as I have not been part of his life.
> Of course, Kurt is very welcome. There are many things I want to ask about him.
> Can I do anything to help?
> If you will send the arrival times I will meet his train.
> > Yours,
> > Piet

Johannes Kerkhoven

Inga's letter only contained information about Kurt's travelling arrangements and the fact that he looked like me.

Anja was sitting across from me at the table.

I handed the letter to her. 'He looks like me.'

'You'll be pleased about that.'

'I certainly am. I've been thinking all sort of things. What if he had been the image of his uncle and Inga was sending him to me as a kind of punishment?'

Inga did not mention my offer of help. I decided that I would talk to Kurt about that. I had no knowledge of what or how much Inga had told our son and that uncertainty made me uneasy. I also wondered how she might have struggled to bring him up by herself. I would have been so happy to help.

The week before Kurt's arrival was a period of frantic and not always rational activity. My mood swung from high excitement to deep depression. I planned all kinds of things we could do together, then decided that it was premature. Let's wait until he arrives. Would the past be there with us? He might hate me. I could understand if he did.

Anja had suggested that Kurt had a right to know what really happened on that Liberation Day nearly twenty years ago.

'I'm ready to let you off the hook, Piet. It's been long enough now.'

'What do you mean?' I asked.

'Well, I've thought about it and I feel that my kids, both Ted and Sofia, are old enough now to take the truth. I don't need to protect them from the truth any longer, certainly not at the cost of your relationship with your son. They should know that it was their mother who killed that German and not that famous Piet van Land.'

'But .–. '

She held up a hand. 'Let me finish. Now that we know you have a son, things are different. God knows what that boy has been told. The truth should come out.'

'I'm not unhappy about the way things have turned out for me.'

'I know that, what about your son? Wouldn't it be fair to let him know that it wasn't his father who killed his uncle? I've come to regret that I was selfish enough to let you take the blame for what I did.'

'My son may not know anything.'

'You don't really believe that.'

'I'm hoping.'

Anja did not answer, she only shook her head.

'Have you thought about what might happen if we did tell the truth now?' I said. Panic overtook me as I thought about the consequences.

'Of course I have. All we have to do is keep it in the family. The ideal way to do this would be for me to talk to your son and if he is sensible enough to agree, to ask him not to broadcast it to the world.'

'Your kids and Maarten, would they want to keep quiet? Maarten might think it a good opportunity to get even with you.'

'Ideally he would not even know, nor should the kids. Besides, Maarten is more interested in his new young wife than in me, I'm certain of that. We've been on amiable terms for some time now. He's happy at last.'

'I don't like it. It's been our secret all these years, why now?'

'I have to do this. I can't live with the guilt any longer. We really must do this regardless of the consequences. Don't you feel that too?'

'No, you've never talked about guilt before, Anja, it's too late to do this.'

Perhaps as we get older it becomes easier to grab hold of happiness. Was I still hoping to have Inga back, now that we have a son? Could time be reversed? Could she be persuaded to forgive me? Was that what I wanted? Anja was being selfish. The most important thing for her seemed to be the need to confess, but why now? I did not want my life to change again. Inga might hate me even more if she learned that I gave her up without a fight in order to protect Anja.

My reactions were powerful and difficult to classify, all I knew was that I did not want the truth to come out.

I felt hot anger against Anja well up inside me. 'God! For how many years have I lived this lie?! You can not do this, you – you – destroyer! My life will be finished. I won't allow it. Unless you give me back my life as it was before you killed Kurt, things must stay as they are. What you did and my reaction to it decided the course my life would take. Now let me live it! I sacrificed my happiness with Inga for you and your children. That was the time you should have come forward, not now!'

If Anja went ahead with her confession, I would have to stop her at any price, I saw now that she had never loved me. Conveniently I had always been there for her. First to dispose of Kurt's body, then, when his body was discovered I was there again, to take the blame for killing him. Both times Anja had got what she wanted. She had avenged her father's death and passed the responsibility for that onto me, and now, because she was feeling uncomfortable, she would complete my destruction.

'What is so horrible is that Inga left me thinking that I had killed her brother. Why didn't you tell her then? The whole thing is – is – .' I had no more words.

Anja did not reply and sat still after my outburst. I had to get away and left the house.

* * *

Cool air has a calming effect, and after walking along the tree-lined roads without sense of time or distance, I realised at last that I was at least four kilometres from home. I hailed a passing taxi.

Anja was in the kitchen and came out when I opened the front door.

I sat down and she sat down opposite me.

'Do you want me to leave?' she said.

I shook my head. 'I only want you to understand.'

'I do now. I didn't know what it meant to you. I did not think it through.' She came and sat next to me. 'I'm preparing your favourite. Chateaubriand. You had better get a firm bottle of red out of your cellar.'

I took her hand. 'You're incorrigible. You'll be the death of me yet,' I was half-serious. Anja made me feel exhausted and I didn't want to deal with her problems any longer. If, when I came back, she had been packed and ready to leave, I would not have stopped her.

CHAPTER THIRTY-SIX

The spare room needed decorating, it looked shabby. I threw out the mattress that Anja and I had meant to replace for some time and bought a new one and new sheets.

Kurt must be about fifteen, I had calculated, so we assumed that he would be a big eater. The freezer compartment of our refrigerator was filled to capacity with steaks, fish, chicken; all the high-protein foods we knew a growing boy needs. Biscuits and chocolate, jam and milk; we stocked up on everything until I was satisfied that we would have enough food for him.

What should a modern father wear? I went to have a haircut and bought some new shirts and trousers. I also rearranged all my appointments so that I would have a free week to spend with him. Anja had decided to go and stay with a friend during his visit, so that he and I would have the opportunity to get to know each other.

On the day of Kurt's arrival I woke up early. I had slept very little, the inside of my mouth felt like hot ash and made me stagger out of bed desperate for a glass of cold water.

Kurt was due to arrive about midday, and there were several hours to fill. I was restless, the shock of having the existence of a son thrust upon me had upset the balance I had managed to achieve during the passing years. I picked up a book and put it down again. I made coffee and adjusted the position of the furniture. Then I made tea. Anja, with my assistance, kept the house clean enough, yet I kept picking up tiny bits of lint from the carpet.

At long last I was standing on the platform at Centraal Station. I was sweating with apprehension. I felt worried on the one hand, yet on the other I was brimming with joy and excitement at meeting him. Would he be like me? I asked myself the biggest question of all again and again: how much does he know about what happened to his uncle?

The large hand of the station clock jumped to the figure ten as the long international express rolled into the station five minutes late and came to a smooth stop. I remembered the day, when I had waited on this very same platform for Inga to arrive.

Doors hissed open and passengers began to pour out, thick crowds of them. Scanning every face I could see no one that I thought could possibly be my son. I was beginning to think that he might not be on the train as the last of the passengers walked past me, none of whom gave me a second glance. Then someone stepped on to the platform out of the very end carriage. He was wearing a full length, black leather coat but was still some distance away and it was difficult to make out his features.

As he came closer, I saw that the young man did not

look anything like me. Could he be Kurt? I squinted to see better and saw that he looked familiar.

He – he looked like – . My God! I shook my head in bewilderment. It was a nightmare. He came closer, and my mouth fell open. He walked up to me and stopped in front of me. It was Kurt! Kurt, the German soldier, that we had buried nearly twenty years before.

'Herr van Land?' The skin of his face was tight and white.

I nodded, stunned, unable to speak.

'I am Kurt Grutz.'

I nodded again and took the hand he extended. His fingers were moist and he withdrew his hand almost on contact.

From the faint smile I saw that he sensed the extent of my confusion. Inga had let this happen without warning me. Did she want to get her revenge, or was she testing me?

'Let me take your bag.' My voice came out hoarse and looking at him, I blinked to stop a tear rolling out of my eye.

He shook his head, and his voice was soft, 'It's not heavy.'

We walked to the car together and I managed to ask him about his trip. I tried to make conversation during the short car ride to the house, asking him about his school, which sport he preferred. Kurt's answers were monosyllabic. It was to be expected. Meeting the man who is your father for the first time, must be difficult. Over the years, he must have wondered about me. This meeting was emotional for both of us and he probably did not want to show that he felt awkward too.

I gradually recovered from the shock of seeing him. I could already feel that establishing a relationship with this boy was going to require a lot of effort on my part. I looked at him sideways and noticed that even his pimples were like his uncle's and I fought revulsion despite the fact that I had no reason to disbelieve that he was my own son.

Once at home, I showed him his room and asked him if he would like to unpack, freshen up maybe, while I prepared a cold lunch. He simply nodded.

Lunch had been ready for some ten minutes, and Kurt still hadn't come out. I went up and knocked on the door.

'Eine Minute, bitte.' His voice sounded strained.

I heard the door open and he came down the stairs and into the living room.

'Please sit …' I began and saw the band with the swastika around his arm.

His face was a deadly white and he looked at me with unmistakable malice. I flinched as I saw the gleam of a small pistol in his hand. I recognised the gun. It was the same one that I had seen at Inga's house in Münster many years before.

'What – what are you doing?' I managed to say.

'You ruined my mother's life and you killed my uncle, my mother's only brother!' He spat the words at me, his mouth twisted. He glared at me through his uncle's eyes.

The gun was very small in his hand, it did not look at all dangerous, more like a cigarette lighter, but it seemed to get bigger as he raised it and pointed it at my chest. His fingertip was curled around the tiny trigger.

How many shots did he have in there?

'Please Kurt,' I held up my hands. My voice sounded, surprisingly, quite calm. 'Let me tell you what really happened.' I took a step towards him, kicking up the corner of my well-worn carpet. Out of habit I smoothed it with my foot, never taking my eyes off him.

'*Nein!* Stay where you are! Don't think I won't shoot. I am the soldier now! I know what happened. Last night my aunt Elsa told me all about it! We know how my uncle died. You pushed the knife right through his ribs, forcing them apart and plunging the blade straight into his heart!'

'I … it wasn't like that. You must listen to me. It was an accident. You must believe me.'

He motioned with the gun for me to stay back. 'The war was over. My uncle should have come home. He had never asked to be a soldier. When you killed him he was almost the same age as I am now and he was not even a Nazi.'

The muscles in his neck throbbed. 'But I am different, I'm sure you have heard of the Neo-Nazis. I am part of the new organization. As a National Socialist I will avenge the callous murder of a German soldier as part of the fight for the new Germany in a new world.'

My eyes went from his taut face to the tiny wavering barrel. He tried to steady the gun, his left hand gripping his right wrist, because he was trembling violently, unable to point the gun straight at my chest.

'Oh Kurt, please let me explain. I did not want your uncle to die. You must believe that. I was only fourteen years old myself at the time, even younger than you are now. The police investigated his death very thoroughly.

State of Guilt

I would have gone to prison if I had been guilty. If I had been able to avoid his death I would have. You don't know how much agony this has caused me all these years. I shall never forget your uncle and those horrible times. Listen to me.'

My God, the thoughts flashed through my head. If he shoots me, his life will be ruined. I could even see the headlines. "Son shoots father. Revenge killing by Neo-Nazi." I wasn't afraid for myself, but for him and for Inga. I must gain time. Calm him down and explain.

'Talk then. I am still going to kill you for what you did to my mother and to my uncle!'

'Your uncle was scared, very scared. He had been separated from the other German soldiers. He was alone on Liberation Day. He was spotted by a mob of people. They were after him, Kurt. They were going to kill him. Everyone was crazy on the day the war ended.' I talked as fast as I could. 'There was pent-up hatred against the German army that had overrun our country. We didn't ask them to come to Holland. They made us suffer. The German army occupied us for five long years. They made our life miserable. Many people died from hunger or were shot by your soldiers or were taken away to die in concentration camps.

'Lies, all filthy lies.'

I knew I had to keep on talking. 'Please understand, Kurt. Some people wanted revenge. Your uncle was running away from them. I saved him from those people. I hid him in our shed. I sent the mob the wrong way, I didn't want him to die, I wanted to help and save him, then he panicked and began to threaten me with an axe, telling me to take off my clothes, so he could put them on instead of his uniform. I was scared and he tried to kill me.'

'Why didn't you give him your clothes. You could have.'

'I wanted to, he never gave me the chance. He was about to split my skull in two. I jumped out of his way and then … he ran into my knife. I held him as he died and then panicked and hid his body in our shed. I didn't know what to do and that same night I buried him in a garden near our house. I felt so bad. I never meant him to die. That's the truth.' I took another step towards my son. 'Please give me the gun.'

He raised the barrel until it pointed at my head. 'I don't believe you. Lying to save yourself won't do you any good.'

'You must believe me, Kurt. You must believe me. I'm your father. I would not lie to you.'

'I don't need a father. You've always lied. You lied to my mother. You ruined her life. You did not care about what happened to her. She had to bring me up all alone and had to pay for everything. You were never there. You never cared. You are a stranger to me. You are not my father and you murdered the only uncle I ever had.'

'I wanted to be with your mother. If I had known about you, nothing would have kept me away. That is the truth.'

'More lies and all of them too late.' The gun was steady now. 'Sixteen years too late.'

'This is not all about your uncle, is it? It's about me, your father. Don't you understand, I want to be your father. Can't you feel how happy I am to have a son? I feel sad, when I think of the times I have missed being with

State of Guilt

you, the growing up, going to school, playing football. Come.'

I took a step towards him again. He didn't seem to notice. Were there tears in his eyes?

We both jumped when the doorbell rang. It rang loudly, insistently, continuously. Someone had got their finger on it, or it had got stuck. I moved towards the door. 'Can I …?'

'Let it ring.'

'Let me tell them to go away.'

I decided to take a chance and took another step towards the hallway door. The little gun exploded, much louder than I had expected. The doorbell stopped ringing. I felt nothing so I assumed he had missed. I stepped through the doorway and another shot rang out, slamming into the thick door as I closed it.

The hallway was only about three meters long, as I crossed it to the front door it felt more like twenty. He didn't fire the gun again and stayed in the living room. My hands were trembling uncontrollably as I opened the front door.

'Inga!'

She pushed past me. 'Kurt, where is Kurt?'

I grabbed her arm. 'Inga, please, he has a gun!'

She pulled herself free and threw herself at the living room door. At the same instant the door swung open, a shot rang out. Inga kept walking towards Kurt who had his eyes shut tight. Her arms stretched out to him. Then, touching him, her legs could no longer support her and she clutched at him but her fingers were unable to hold on and she slid to the floor.

Horror distorted Kurt's face. 'Mum!'

His cry tore my heart in two. The gun fell to the floor. I carried Inga to the settee and phoned for an ambulance. They arrived within minutes.

Kurt clung to Inga. 'Please, Mummy, I'm sorry, I'm sorry. Please don't die.'

She managed to give him a weak smile, 'Forgive …' she whispered and closed her eyes.

In my agony I wished that he had not missed me when I went to answer the door. Then Inga would still be alive. Within minutes I heard the police siren. The armband Kurt had been wearing was lying on the floor half showing the swastika. I picked it up and put it in my pocket.

Very briefly I told the policemen what had happened and they gently made Kurt stand up. The ambulance men carefully lifted Inga onto a stretcher. The police led Kurt away, and as he went out, his eyes glittered at me, alive with hatred.

I walked behind the stretcher as it was negotiated into the hallway. A car with German number plates was parked halfway up the driveway. A small silent crowd had gathered on the pavement outside my home. In the ambulance, as I looked at Inga's white face, tears began to flow from my eyes. Why did this terrible thing have to happen? After I had allowed myself a tiny bit of hope for happiness after learning of Kurt's existence.

Inga opened her eyes several times and looked at me with a hint of a smile around her lips. It was as if time fell away. I felt a surge of love for her. She had not changed at all, save that her dark hair had a few strands of grey in it.

'Please don't leave me again,' I asked her silently when

the ambulance arrived at the hospital and they wheeled her away.

Two policemen came up to me. They had been waiting in the reception area of the hospital.

'Sir, do you feel up to making a statement? It might even help.' One of them said.

I nodded and felt tears flooding my eyes. They let me be for a minute or two and after I had blown my nose hard, I was ready. 'Such a waste,' I said.

'In your own words, please tell us what happened,' he said calmly.

As best as I could I told them about Kurt's arrival.

'This was a terrible accident.' I kept having to stop as my tears threatened to start flowing again. Then I noticed a young doctor coming towards me. His face was explicit. I knew at once that Inga had died.

'I'm sorry,' he said. 'We did all we could.'

I started to shake violently, and one of the policemen put his arm around my shoulder. 'No, no!' I screamed inside my head. I looked at him without being able to focus my eyes on him. 'I can't go on.'

'That's quite all right, Sir. We'll contact you tomorrow for your statement. Can we give you a lift home?'

I shook my head and looked at the doctor. 'Please?'

He knew what I was asking and nodded. 'If you can wait a little while you will be able to see her.'

CHAPTER THIRTY-SEVEN

The streets were dark now, glistening and whipped by a fierce wet wind. My body was numb, my mind was numb

To meet my son and have him threaten me, seeing Inga again and, seconds later, see her collapse from the bullet that was intended for me, was too much. There was a look of total horror and disbelief on Kurt's face as he tried to grasp what he had done, his mouth open in a silent scream and his eyes full of terror.

I kept walking without direction until I shivered and realised I was drenched. I kept walking.

The pain inside my chest and head was unbearable. Why couldn't I have let him shoot me. Inga hadn't deserved to die like this and I did not deserve to live. I had made an irreparable mess of my life.

Aunt Elsa told me later that she had told Kurt about his uncle's death, after he had kept pressing her. Later she had become worried and had rung Inga the following morning.

'I want to kill him,' Kurt had said to Aunt Elsa.

State of Guilt

Inga had decided at once that she must stop him. As she packed a few clothes, she thought of the small pistol that Kurt had spotted in her wardrobe some little time earlier. She had told him to put it back where he had found it. She finished packing, frantically checked and found the gun missing and knew that Kurt had taken it with him. She drove as fast as she dared, wanting to get to my house before Kurt's arrival. Aunt Elsa also told me that Inga had never stopped loving me and that she had wanted so much to come back to me even though she believed I had killed her brother.

I kept walking the streets aimlessly. I thought of phoning Anja. She was always strong. Maybe she could help me. But I wanted to hate her and never see her again, get her out of my life. Go to another country, buy an airline ticket tomorrow to anywhere, disappear and begin a new life, without Anja, without my family, without anyone. Take my camera gear and get out. Yet I knew that even that would not work. Nothing would ever make me forget what had happened.

I wanted to lie down and go to sleep, anywhere and not wake up again. I could jump into the canal. I looked up to see where I was. The water was two minutes away. Jump with my mouth wide open and let the water flow into my lungs. I knew that I was not brave enough to do that. I would have to go on and on and forever see Inga and Kurt during that ghastly moment. Kurt, my son.

I stopped. What will happen to him? He will be charged. I must help him, be there for him.

Albert, I thought. The only one I could go to was Albert. Ten minutes later I rang his door bell and quickly an upstairs window opened.

'Just a minute,' he said, when he saw it was me.

His front door opened and I saw that he was dressed. 'I heard the news, Piet. I went round to your house. There was no answer.'

'I ...'

'Come in.'

I stepped inside his hallway and stopped. Kurt! He suddenly sprang back into my mind. My son! What had I been thinking of. I am not alone. I must go to him.

'I can't come in. The police have taken Kurt away. I must go to him. He's my son.'

Albert's flat was not far from the police station and I decided to go there at once. Maybe they would let me see him. I wanted to let him know that he could depend on me. That I did not blame him, that I knew that what had happened had been a ghastly accident.

'I'll come with you.' Albert said and reached for the umbrella stand. 'Here, at least take one of these.'

Carla appeared at the top of the stairs. 'Albert?'

'I won't be long. I'll be with Piet.'

He ran after me as I was already walking fast through the unrelenting rain and wind.

'Do you want to talk?'

'No.' I shook my head and we walked on in silence.

The policeman at the front desk was polite but firm. 'It will have to wait until the morning. The prisoner is asleep.'

The warmth inside the police station made me realise how cold I felt and I shivered again. My clothes were soaked right through. My trousers were clinging to my legs.

State of Guilt

'You'd better get yourself home, Sir. Get out of those clothes and into a hot bath.'

'Yes, thank you,' I answered and looked at Albert. I knew that I could not sleep in the house tonight.

'Come and stay in my spare room.'

'Thanks, Albert. You're always there but I'll sleep on the sofa in the studio.'

'Okay.' He didn't press me. He probably thought it would be simpler. Carla would not be overjoyed to see me. Albert walked me home. Again we did not talk, and I appreciated the fact that he did not pester me with questions.

'Thanks, Albert,' I said at the studio door, 'and, sorry I woke you.'

'What are brothers for?'

I let him hug me for a moment and went inside.

CHAPTER THIRTY-EIGHT

The streets were dry except for the large pool of black water on the corner of our street. My left shoe filled up as I stepped into it, crossing on my way to the police station. One of the officers sitting at the desk behind the counter looked up and I explained that I wanted to see my son.

'Name?'

'Van Land. But my son's name is Grutz. Kurt Grutz.'

He looked at me, opened his mouth as if about to ask a question, then he pursed his lips, turned round and disappeared behind the door at the rear of the room.

I drummed my fingers on the edge of the counter as I waited, until a second policeman sitting at his desk stopped writing and looked up.

'Sorry.' I stopped and put my hand in my pocket, and realised I was rattling the coins in it.

After some minutes, the door at the rear opened. The policeman shook his head as he came back in.

'I'm sorry, Mr. Grutz does not want to see anyone. In fact, he says he has no father, and Sir, you must excuse me, it was difficult to make him understand me. He only speaks German. There is also the surnames. What did you say your name was?'

'Van Land, Piet van Land.'

'That's what I thought. The prisoner's name is Grutz. You said you are related?'

'Yes. Please, I can explain all that. His mother was living here in Holland and I, we … please believe me. I am his father. So could you please go and ask him again. He is distressed. If you could please tell him that I love him very much and that I will give him all the help I can.'

He shrugged almost imperceptibly and threw a sideways glance at his colleague who did not look up or stop writing. 'Very well, Sir.' He went back again to where I supposed the cells were.

This time he did not take very long. As before, he shook his head. He no longer looked sympathetic. 'Very sorry, Sir. He wants to be left alone.'

'But – '

'Sorry, Sir. I suggest you accept the prisoner's wishes.'

This time his colleague did look up, pen held still.

I tried again later that day, and the next day and the next, until I did not have to ask the policemen anything. As I came in one of them would get up and go to tell Kurt that I was there. My son never changed his mind.

After he was transferred to prison, I attended each weekly visiting hour for several months, and never once managed to catch a glimpse of him.

He stood between two policemen at Inga's funeral and again I tried to talk to him. He avoided looking at me until he left. As he walked past, he looked at me with a look of such burning hatred that I winced.

I was pleased that I had insisted that Anja stay away from the funeral. Anja had not heard about the shooting of Inga until the next morning. She had come back to me immediately. 'That poor boy. How must he feel?'

I had no answer for her. How could I have? That poor boy! I had not yet told Anja that my son was the exact double of his uncle. She felt responsible for Inga's death, but how would she feel if she saw the boy? I did not want her to know, not yet. He was my son, and Anja was not likely to meet him for some time.

Anja realised how much Inga had meant to me. It was not that I had not loved Anja; I had. However, right from our first kiss and the first exploration of each other's bodies, Anja had been the instigator, the leader, and I had been the willing participant. When for some reason we were apart during our teenage years, I had trusted her. I used to miss Anja so much that I felt ill with longing for her and thought I must be going insane. I was unable to concentrate on anything, wondering what she was doing. I couldn't be happy until we were together again. Though Anja often told me she loved me and wanted to be with me, I felt that she might be equally happy without me.

Once I met Inga I realised that it was possible to have a different kind of love. Inga and I were equal partners in life and happiness. It was only now, that I had seen her and lost her again that I realised how much I had cared for her.

* * *

Anja did not mention again that she wanted to tell Kurt the truth about his uncle's death. I sensed that it was still smouldering inside her. Inga's death had shocked her and she felt responsible.

'Did you ever tell her that you did *not* kill her brother?' Anja asked.

I shook my head. 'I did not. That was my choice. Telling the truth would not bring back the German soldier and can you imagine what the newspapers would do? It would be unbearable. So forget about changing events. It would destroy our lives.'

She knew that I could never again love her as totally as I had done in the past and that we would never be able to recreate what we had experienced when we first said we loved each other.

Because Anja had chosen Maarten, I had felt betrayed. The pain those feelings had given me had disappeared. I no longer depended on Anja to make me happy. That was liberating and in itself a source of some relief from my despair. Our roles were reversed. She needed me more than I needed her. I could live without her now and she knew it. My dark days had nothing to do with Anja but everything about my loss of Inga.

CHAPTER THIRTY-NINE

Kurt's trial was days away and it would be the first time Anja would see him, so I wanted to prepare her.

'Anja, there's something about my son that you should know.'

'What on earth do you mean, Piet?'

'It's about how he looks.'

'Is there something wrong with him? Is he handicapped? Or – why don't you get to the point, Piet?'

'Well …' I still wanted to delay telling her, prepare her. 'When I saw him get off the train, I was shocked. You see,' I had to go on and spoke quickly, 'he is the image of his uncle. It was as if the German soldier had got out of his grave and had come back to get us.'

Anja said nothing. She frowned.

'Are you all right?'

She nodded slowly. 'Yes. I'm all right. I'm glad you've told me. So he looks like his uncle, and why shouldn't he? His mother must have been pleased.'

'He looks exactly like his uncle, except, he is perhaps a fraction taller.'

State of Guilt

'Frankly, darling Piet, I can't recall *what* that soldier looked like. The memory of his face is completely gone so what your son looks like does not have any relevance for me. After all, I only saw the German soldier for some very brief moments.'

When she eventually saw Kurt, she remarked that she couldn't see any great likeness between my son and the boy's uncle. 'The boy's got brown eyes. The soldier's eyes were grey I seem to recall.'

It was curious; he did look different to me during the trial. His face seemed longer, more like my own, there were no pimples to be seen and his height was not far short of mine. Was it possible that I had imagined the likeness between the living and the dead Kurt?

Once the trial started I was only concerned for Kurt. To see him sitting in the courtroom, motionless, staring in front of him, his eyes, his face, totally without expression, was agony. It was as if he did not realise where he was or what was happening. The charges were read by the prosecutor first in Dutch and then translated into German. Even then he showed no emotion. He would only stand up or sit down when Veilinga whispered in his ear or motioned to him.

Without Kurt's knowledge, I had engaged Veilinga, the lawyer who had defended me. I was summoned to give evidence for the prosecution. Hubert Veilinga had told me to simply tell the truth. 'There was no intent to kill his mother. That will be established very quickly.'

The president of the court said to me, 'Please tell us how the event appeared to you. Did the accused produce a weapon?'

I looked at Hubert, who nodded. 'Yes', I said, 'Kurt

did have a gun in his hand. When it went off, his eyes were closed. I was standing immediately behind his mother and saw the horror on his face when he realised what had happened. It was indescribable.'

As I looked at my son, I still saw no emotion on his face and I wished I had taken the blame on his behalf. I could have taken the gun when he dropped it and wiped his fingerprints off it. Then I would have helped him carry some of the excruciating pain and horror he must still be feeling after what had happened and compensate a little for what had happened between Inga and me. I had not thought of it, my first concern had been to get help for Inga after she was shot.

Hubert had warned me that Kurt would have to serve a sentence, and he was right. When the court was ready to pass judgment two weeks later, the three judges agreed that Inga's death had been an accident, but because Kurt had brought a fully loaded gun to the scene of the crime, there could have been intent.

> The Court:
> - declares that all of the the aforegoing evidence demonstrates that the suspect has broken the law and is therefore punishable;
> - sentences the suspect to four years' detention.

My breath stopped and there was a humming from the public gallery.

'With good behaviour he will be out within three years,' Hubert assured me. It was little consolation. Three years!

CHAPTER FORTY

The strain and sadness of the court case and Kurt's subsequent sentence was not lightened by my relationship with Anja. Recent events had changed both of us.

I had sold the high street photography business. My prints and books of my photographs brought in enough income for us to live comfortably and being absorbed in the work made it easier to cope.

Anja and I began to work together. We photographed landscapes, at least I did. Anja became interested in portraiture. Not photographs of the type I used to do in the studio. She looked for character. She loved finding faces that "tell a story", the social status of the sitters was irrelevant to her.

Our work led to more exhibitions and more books. The first book Anja and I did together was received very well, and established our reputation as a team.

My dear brother Albert lived at a convenient distance so he and I met occasionally. He loved to remind me how we had shared the war years together. Like everyone else, he still thought that I was a killer. How little he knew me.

Didn't he know that I would much rather run away from violence than confront it?

The rest of my family almost became strangers. My sister Tina, and all the uncles and aunts, were quite happy to avoid me. It was always painful to see Mum and Dad trying to be natural and I would have loved to tell them the truth. I thought of leaving a letter to be opened only after my own and Anja's death, and I could almost hear the prattle. It would be a selfish thing to do, an attempt to make them think better of me when I was dead, that is, if I did not outlive them all.

The time for Kurt's release came closer. It was sad and difficult to have a son who refused to see me or accept any help from me. I intended to keep trying to make him change his mind.

Anja was concerned. 'Kurt showed so much hatred during the trial when he looked at you. I'm worried that he might turn up here with his head full of revenge and try to do something silly. Let me go and see if he won't talk to me.'

Predictably Kurt refused to see Anja. We talked to his parole officer to ask for his professional help. He said that he had tried to persuade Kurt that he should see his visitors and suggested that we accept things as they were and let the matter rest for the time being. He wanted to be reassuring. 'I'm convinced that he blames nobody but himself for what has happened. He knows he pulled that trigger and he's paying for it. I feel that all he wants now is to get on with his life. I hope that in time he will be able to learn to live with what happened.'

'How can I make him see that I love him and need him as much as he needs me? That I want to help him

State of Guilt

start the rest of his life? Even if he does not want to meet me, maybe I could help him financially.'

'Although I do sympathise,' the officer said, 'there is nothing more you can do at the moment. I suggest, however, that you try and keep in touch with him, send him the occasional letter, and I'll talk to him again and attempt to make him change his mind. However, that young man is very determined to live by himself, without having anything to do with you. So perhaps you ought to respect that. Besides, he doesn't seem to be alone. He gets regular letters from Germany and some from here in Holland as well. There have been visitors that he has agreed to see.'

'Does he intend to go to Germany on his release? And who are those visitors?'

'To your first question, no, he doesn't, that's why I'm involved. He said he would like to stay in Holland for some time with friends. Perhaps get a job. I don't really know who those friends are. They may be Dutch as Kurt has learnt our language reasonable well.'

Anja and I didn't know what to make of that. Should we be grateful? Did I dare hope that Kurt, despite his refusals to see me, wanted to be close to me or was there another reason? Would he try to kill me again?

Aunt Elsa came to see us once more. She was thin and frail now, and I could not help recalling the weekend in Münster when I had first met her and she had been so vivacious. She was determined that she would be there for Kurt when he was released. She was the only link I had with my son. We did not tell her that Kurt might stay in Holland for some time. We did not know this for certain and didn't want to worry her.

Had Kurt loaded guilt onto me? I hoped for his sake that he would be able to accept that Inga's death was an accident and that his uncle's death was the result of the terrible war. If he could do that his hate might slowly disappear. Was I hoping for the impossible?

'Don't give up,' Aunt Elsa begged me. 'Give him time. He is still so young. I'm certain that we will convince him in the end. We must. That boy needs you more than he knows.'

I hugged her, 'I won't give up,' I said. 'How can I? He's my son. He's my only link with Inga. He's part of her and part of me.'

CHAPTER FORTY-ONE

Kurt made no contact with me on his release. As predicted he did serve less than three years of his sentence. I told myself that I should get used to the idea that I might never hear from him. To have a son and not be able to show him your love is difficult.

Because she had children herself, Anja understood how I felt. Maarten, her ex-husband had always been very careful not to hit Anja in front of the children and she was grateful for that. She did not want them to think of their father as she knew him. She was protecting her children and for that same reason she was grateful that they did not see her as someone who had killed another person. Yet both her children, Ted and Sofia, had not forgiven Anja for walking out on them as they called it. 'But one day they'll come back to me. When they're older.'

We kept busy with our work. I with my landscapes and Anja with her character portraits. If she spotted anyone with a face that interested her, she would ask that person to pose for her. Her subjects ranged from housewives to prostitutes and from businessmen to beggars.

We both had our separate though to some extent common interests.

The way Anja had taken up portraiture was a joy. She liked beggars and tramps best.

'They show more of their character than most of us do.'

She always paid them for their time, and had no trouble getting subjects.

'Meet Victor, Piet,' she said one afternoon, coming into the studio followed by the dirtiest, smelliest individual I had ever encountered.

I recognised the dirt-blackened face as the subject of a portrait she had taken the previous day, sitting on a park bench. We had printed the negatives up that morning and I found this portrait easily her best. The print showed dirt and dilapidation on the subject, but despite the grime, through it, a once handsome face could seen. Shrewd intelligence and amusement beamed out of his dark eyes.

I held my breath so as not to inhale the stench that surrounded him like a no entry zone.

'Pleased to meet you, Victor,' I lied and without thinking held out my hand and as I did so, wished I hadn't.

The man vigorously rubbed his palm on the ancient mud-grey jacket he was wearing and grabbed my hand. Surprisingly there was not enough grime on it to weld his hand instantly to mine.

I looked at Anja, a question on my face.

'Victor has come to pose for me,' she said lightly.

'You took his picture yesterday, did you not?' I said,

'Why bring him to the studio? You won't do a better one in here.'

'Exactly, Piet. I thought I would do a series of portraits of gentlemen and ladies who live on the street in –,' instead of the word filth I expected, Anja said after a minimal pause, 'in unfortunate circumstances. I take their picture in their "natural" environment,' she glanced at Victor, who nodded brightly, 'then I have them clean themselves up and take their portrait again in the studio, all neat and nice.' She waited for my answer. 'Not a good idea?'

Damn it, I thought. I was instantly reminded of my "Girl series". Ignoring the stab of regret I felt, I smiled. 'Anja, you're amazing.'

Victor shuffled towards the door in his over-sized boots. 'Is this my exit?' He directed his question at Anja, ignoring me.

'It's okay,' I said, waving my hand at him. 'I think it's a wonderful idea. I can see a whole series now. *Tramps are People,* or whatever you'll call it.' He took a step back towards me and I was overwhelmed by his stench and made a coughing sound. 'Maybe we'd better get on with it then.'

'Can you, uh, show Victor where the bathroom is and so on?' Anja said, smiling sweetly.

I blew up my cheeks and let the air escape. 'Of course.' Then to Victor who did not seem embarrassed at all, 'Follow me.'

'My God, we'll have to get the place fumigated after this.' I almost said aloud as we went into the house. I stood aside to let him enter the bathroom. 'Wait a second. Don't lock yourself in yet.' I'd already decided that he would never wear those clothes again. I handed him a plastic bag. Put your clothes in here please.'

I left him to it and heard the bolt slide home on the inside of the door. Back in the studio Anja was busy setting up lights. 'So,' I said.

She looked up. 'So?'

'So what's he going to wear?'

'I uh, I thought since he is about your size, you wouldn't mind if he borrowed some of your clothes, would you?' She folded her arms. Anja had already decided what would happen.

I burst out laughing. 'You're the limit. You expect me to give him my clothes?'

'Not your best suit, of course.'

'Oh, thank you.' I laughed again.

'Didn't you say last Sunday that the wardrobe was getting too small?'

'Yes, I did. Does that mean … oh, hell, why not? I do have far too many clothes.'

While I was going through my wardrobe, I was reminded of the clothes I had given the German soldier many years earlier. I chose some underwear, a shirt and a suit that always hung a little loosely on me, also a pair of socks and a tie that had been a present from Albert and I felt was too loud, even for my taste. I added a pair of shoes. Good quality, though I never knew why I had bought them. I don't liked brogues.

In the bathroom Victor began to sing in a surprisingly pleasant tenor voice. 'La donna è mobile, come piuma al vento!'

'Open up, Caruso!' I called out.

The bolt slid back and a grinning, dripping head

appeared around the door. I handed him the clothes. 'Hand me the bag with everything you took off, please.'

I took the bag between thumb and index finger, and, holding my nose with my free hand, I immediately went to the rubbish bin at the back of the house.

Half an hour later Victor walked back into the studio. I knew it was Victor. It had to be but the change was unbelievable.

'Bloody hell!' I called out.

The suit was made for him. His shoulders were obviously that little bit broader than mine and the tie was suddenly no longer too loud.

'Thank you, Sir,' Victor nodded at me.

'I knew it,' Anja was happy. 'Come and sit here, Victor, you gentleman you.'

Back very straight, he walked over to where she wanted him to sit. He looks great, I thought, confident, even a little smug. His black hair, greying at the temples and combed back now, gave him a distinguished look. He held his chin higher than most people would and looked down at the world along his now clean Roman nose. A handsome man, a few years older than me. As he went past me, instead of the powerful, foul odour, I smelled my most expensive after shave. The one I only ever used on special occasions.

'Piet, I feel we ought to have a pocket handkerchief here, don't you?'

'Of course.' I was already on my way.

Needless to say the portrait session was a success. When she was finished it was late afternoon, so Anja invited Victor to stay for dinner. Somehow I had known this would happen all along.

Johannes Kerkhoven

The dinner was not the disaster I had envisaged. If any of our friends had visited us unexpectedly, they would have been delighted with Victor's conversation, as both Anja and I were.

'What interesting times we live in,' Victor said, holding his glass of burgundy against the light. He adjusted the jacket he was wearing, 'yes, quite interesting times.'

'Tell us about yourself,' Anja asked.

'There isn't much to tell. I'm simply an actor who is resting, no longer in demand. Ten years ago it was different.' He stood up.

'I'll show thee the best springs, I'll pluck thee berries.
I'll fish for thee, and get thee wood enough.
A plague upon the tyrant that I serve!
I'll bear him no more sticks, but follow thee,
Thou wondrous man.'

He was addressing me.

'Shakespeare?' We clapped.

'*The Tempest*. Alas, dear friends, there is no call for great drama now. We had eggs thrown at us during the last Shakespeare rehearsal I attended. I shall never know why. There is more violence and sex in "The Bard's" theatre than in these modern wishy-washy plays. It is a case of youth aching to replace their elders. Pity. They have so much to learn.'

Towards the end of the evening it was not clear to me what would happen next. After all, when someone has just been an entertaining dinner guest at your house, and is wearing your clothes, how do you tell him to go and sleep under a bridge?

'For tonight, you may sleep in the studio.' I didn't want to think beyond this.

'I would not think of it.' He stood up. 'I have a very comfortable spot which I call my own. Besides, people are expecting me.'

'Victor,' Anja said, 'it's raining hard. Do you want to ruin the clothes that Piet has lent you?'

'I do apologise, Piet. I shall take them off immediately. Where are the trusty garments I came in?'

'Gone.' Under no circumstances was I going to let those putrid rags back inside my house.

'See?' Anja said.

'In that case I surrender.'

When I entered the studio the next morning I was welcomed by the smell of fresh coffee and the floor was cleaner than it had been for some time. Victor had managed to use some of our backdrops to curtain off a corner behind which the sofa now stood.

Anja was not going to throw him out and, although I thought about it, I did not have the heart to do it either. In any case, Victor had already decided that he was going to adopt us. In no time at all he made me realise that I could do with someone to look after details in the studio, deliveries and so on, and that he, Victor, was the man to do all that for us. Together we built a small comfortable room at the rear of the studio.

CHAPTER FORTY-TWO

Everyone has a past, and Victor was no exception. We included his two portraits in our next exhibition and a few days after the opening an anonymous letter was left at the gallery addressed to Anja. It stated that the man in the portrait was Victor Zoeters, that he had served in the Waffen-SS during the war in a unit made up of Dutch volunteers, and that he had fought on the Russian front with distinction as early as 1942. After the war his unit surrendered and he had served a three months prison sentence.

We decided not to confront Victor with this information. 'Even if it is true,' I said, 'he has done his time and what more can we ask of him?'

I expected Anja, who had revenged her father by killing a German in cold blood, to be furious and instantly start screaming for Victor to get out, but to my amazement she merely nodded. Had she been able to let go of her hatred for the Nazis?

'The name Zoeters rings a bell somewhere. Have we met anyone by that name?'

'Not that I remember,' said Anja.

One morning, not long after the arrival of the anonymous letter, I entered the studio. There was no answer to my 'Good morning' call, so I crossed the floor and knocked on Victor's door. Still no answer. Could he be ill? Then I noticed the key in the lock. Again I knocked, again no response. I opened the door and saw that his bed was made up to its usual, military precision. At the head was an envelope addressed to me. "Thank you for everything", was all it said.

I shook my head not quite believing what I read. I thought was happy with us.

When I went back into the house and showed Victor's note to Anja she did not seem surprised.

'He must have a good reason, so why couldn't he have talked it over with us? Do you have any ideas?' I asked her.

She rubbed her chin as if to massage the answer from there. 'Who knows. There was a letter for him, the first and only one, around the same time as I received the anonymous one about him at the gallery. Could Victor have received threats to expose him? If so, he might have thought, before they do that I'll disappear.'

'Yes. Who knows? Do people still bear a grudge after how many years now?'

'That's not so difficult to imagine,' Anja said.

'I suppose it's easy enough,' I said, puzzled by her casual tone of voice. Had Victor been able to charm her to the extent that she was able to overlook his past?

Anja thought he might miss being a tramp. 'These chaps like their freedom. Maybe he was bored. The job he did for us didn't exactly tax his abilities.'

'That's true. Still, I'm angry. Ungrateful bugger. We really know nothing about him, do we?'

I knew Victor had been out for a drink with Albert the day before his disappearance, so I asked my brother if Victor had said anything about leaving us.

'No. Nothing. I'm as surprised as you are. He asked me lots of questions about you. How you came to be a hero and so on. He wanted to know everything.'

'And you told him. Did you tell him about Inga and my son?'

'I shouldn't have?'

I shrugged. 'No matter. It's common knowledge.'

But it did matter. We had become used to having Victor around. I missed him and I was disappointed that he had left so suddenly.

After a week we stopped talking about Victor. There were trips to plan for our next book. Another week went by when, as suddenly as he had disappeared, Victor walked in again.

'Hello, Piet.'

'Victor! What the hell is the meaning of this? Where have you been?' I felt anger rise up in me.

'Piet, I'm sorry. I couldn't do anything else. I've got a long story to tell you.'

'You bet you have. You can't do this to us. Maybe you can also tell me who Victor Zoeters is.' As I said the name it flashed into my consciousness. There had been a Lud Zoeters in my class at School. We had been friendly. He disappeared from my life when I was about eight years old.

'Let me explain. First of all, I'm sorry that I caused you distress. I did not mean to do that. Yes, I did change my name after the war. If I hadn't I would never have been able to work as an actor. And yes, I could have told you about it, when you offered to look after me, because again, yes, I did remember you as my younger brother's friend. However I was concerned about how you would react. After all, we traitors, as you call us, expect to be ostracized for ever.'

At that moment Anja came out of the darkroom.

'Victor!' Anja dropped the print she was holding and ran up to him and threw her arms about him. 'Where have you been you naughty man?'

He looked at me over Anja's shoulder. 'I've met your son.'

I didn't hear what he said. I was still angry with him.

'Piet!' Anja yelled.

Victor said again, louder. 'Piet, I've met your son.'

My mouth fell open, not believing what I heard. 'What did you say?'

He disengaged himself from Anja's arms. 'I bring you news from your son. He's well and wants to meet you.'

My God! I began to shake. 'But how …? What do you mean?'

'Let me start at the beginning. Your brother Albert told me everything that happened to you in the past, yes even about your son, too. So I decided to help you.'

'You did?'

'Yes, I decided to effect the reconciliation, correction, *con*ciliation between you and your son. I knew where you were, so all I had to do was find your son Kurt. Your brother Albert gave me all the information I needed for that. He told me that Kurt liked to think of himself as a Neo-Nazi. A German Neo-Nazi who's been in gaol for killing his mother and who has friends here in Holland isn't hard to find. I've had some dealings with Neo-Nazis myself.'

He drew in his breath and whistled. 'They're a nasty lot. They did approach me to join their movement. I sent them packing. They're of the opinion that Hitler was right about killing Jews, Gypsies and handicapped people.'

'We know all that, Victor,' I said.

'Oh, yes, of course,' he held up his hands.

His eyes were smiling as he went on. 'Well, through their network I soon found out that while in prison, your son became a member of a group in Groningen. Their "Führer" was very dismissive about Kurt, "too soft", but he gave me Kurt's address in Münster and hey presto; three days after I left here I was talking to him. So you understand that I couldn't let you know what I planned to do, in case I failed.'

Anja's eyes were beaming at him. 'You didn't fail, did you?'

I grabbed his arm. 'Go on, man, what happened?'

'He lives in a house by himself, and at first he didn't want to have anything to do with me. I even gave him the Nazi salute. He didn't like that. It took all my talents to persuade him that he needed me. What a splendid performance I gave. I'd like to see some of these young actors—'

I interrupted him. 'Never mind that. Go on.'

'—do that.' Victor finished his sentence.

'How is he? Is he well? Does he work? God man, tell me. Tell me. Everything!'

'Yes, your son is well, Piet. I could see that he was

State of Guilt

lonely. He cried when he told me that his aunt Elsa had died a few weeks earlier.'

'That is sad. We didn't know. She wrote to us not so long ago.'

Victor did not speak for some moments. 'Well, I talked to him for hours and eventually persuaded him that he should trust me, that he needn't be alone. However, he was afraid that you wouldn't want to see him. It had been a long time and after his behaviour he felt that he had no right to contact you.'

'What nonsense!' I called out.

'I think I finally made him believe that,' Victor went on. 'He didn't want to come with me, so he sends you a message.' He reached in his pocket and handed me an envelope.

'Thank God,' Anja said.

I took the envelope and looked at both of them. Victor standing there, smiling. I slowly opened the envelope, took out the single sheet of paper and unfolded it. *Dear Father,* it said at the top. Kurt, it really is from Kurt! I kept looking at those two words: *"Dear Father."*

Blinking stopped the forming tears. 'I ... I'll go and read it in the house. Do you mind?'

'Of course not,' said Anja. 'I'll make coffee. Don't be forever. We want to know what's in the letter, too.'

Dear Father,
Victor has persuaded me that I may contact you. He helped me write this letter. I am very sorry about my behaviour in the past, but Victor said the past is gone and that you would always be

there for me, so now I am ready to take you at your word.

Here I had to stop reading. I gasped as sobs closed my throat. Then I held the letter up again.

I would like to come and live in Holland and I need help to establish myself. Victor was certain that I could depend on you and he has promised to let me know what your reaction to this letter is.
Your son,
Kurt

I put the letter down and sat still. Tears were running down my cheeks. I stood up and went back to the studio.

Anja looked at me over her reading glasses. There were tears in her eyes too as she stood up and put her arms around me. 'At last, Piet, at last.'

I nodded, swallowing hard. 'Yes, at last. This letter is so honest. It must have been painful for him to write it. Wonderful Aunt Elsa. She knew that she would convince him eventually. She's passed away and that makes me very sad. How lonely Kurt must have felt after she had gone. Yet, reading his letter, I feel that everything that happened to him has made him stronger. That comes out clearly in the way he writes.'

I handed it to her. "You must read it.'
'What will you do next?'
'Write to him, phone him, contact him. I'll try and phone him at once, shall I? Now, immediately?'

Anja smiled. 'Yes, I'd do that if I were you.'

'That won't be necessary,' Victor said. 'He's waiting, Piet.'

'Waiting where?'

'He's quite close by.'

'He's here? Here in Utrecht, where?'

Victor nodded, 'It wasn't easy to persuade him, but yes, Piet, he's here. He's having a coffee a few minutes away.'

'Where, Victor, where!?' I felt like shaking him.

'In *De Drie Bellen,* the café on the corner of …'

I ran to the door. 'I know where it is,' I said and was on my way.

CHAPTER FORTY-THREE

When I stood in front of the café and was about to open the door, I stopped for some seconds. My God. What will I say to my son. How does he see me now? I pushed against the door and entered. This is it. My life is about to change.

The café was almost empty and I spotted Kurt at once, sitting at a table with an overnight bag on the floor beside him. He stood up and extended his hand. His handshake was firm now, not as it had been – was it already four years ago? He looked thinner, straighter, manly. I could no longer see any resemblance between my son and his uncle. Instead he looked at me with Inga's brown eyes. I detected no hate in them.

'Hello, Kurt,' I said.

'Hello, Father.'

I liked being called Father.

We looked at each other. His eyes were pleading. I took a step towards him and threw my arms around him. We stood like this for some moments and I stepped back, my hands on his shoulders. We were smiling at each other and sat down.

The waiter, smiling too, was adjusting the table cloth on the next table.

'Would you like a coffee?'

'I – yes, thank you, Kurt.' I sat down opposite him.

'One more coffee please,' he said to the waiter.

'Very well, Sir.'

'You look well,' Kurt said at the same moment as I said, 'You look well.'

We both laughed and I was glad. At once I felt relaxed and I could see the tension leaving his face.

'I read your letter, Kurt.'

'You didn't mind?'

'Mind? I was glad, very glad.' I glanced at the waiter. 'Thank you,' I said as he set the coffee down in front of me. I turned back to Kurt. 'You are the most important person in my life right now.'

He did not answer that and I put it down to embarrassment. 'Tell me what you've been doing since, uh, since I last saw you,' I said.

A hint of a smile crossed his face. 'I've been doing many things, mainly trying to grow up a little. The accident with Mother made me want to die. It was so unfair that she died. She was the most wonderful person in my life, and always will be.'

He had grown up. It must have taken a long time and a lot of soul searching for him to be able to mention Inga's death like this.

'I do understand that. I loved her too, more than I've ever loved anyone before or since.' To mask my emotion I took a sip of coffee.

'I was very angry when I first began to serve my sentence. When I came out of prison I went to stay with a Dutch friend I'd met there. He was a Neo-Nazi as I thought I was. At the time it was good for me to have someone there.'

'Of course.' I picked up my coffee again.

'This man, he called himself Heinrich, was older than me and we had to call him our Führer. We talked about everything that was wrong with our lives and the world. His house in Groningen was like a headquarters of the local Neo-Nazis. I liked some of them, but others I disliked very much.'

'You didn't want to go home to Germany?'

'I wanted to be away from Aunt Elsa. My friend was exciting. He told me that he was working for a new unified Germany, with Holland being a very important part of it, like a province. Everybody would be equal and speak German as a common language. He said that as early as the seventeenth century there had been border disputes, and large parts of Holland should be German. We believed in the NSDAP programme of 1920, which advocates Germany for the Germans.'

I shook my head. 'It's amazing how the average person knows so little about history and what's happening.'

Kurt stroked the red-checked table cloth, removing an imaginary crumb. 'It seems ridiculous now, but at that time I wanted to be part of the movement because of my friend, not because I accepted all of it. I can see that now. We argued a lot. The group wanted only pure Aryans in the new Germany as Hitler had and they were prepared to be ruthless. Heinrich said that the churches too had always believed in purity of race. What he said seemed reasonable. Even if some of the principles might be unpleasant for some people, they would be justified if they were for the greater good of the New Germany.'

'Did you have to do things you didn't agree with?' I asked.

'We did scare some Gypsies. We threw Molotov cocktails into their camp. I went with them even though I felt uneasy about it. Heinrich and the others persuaded me by saying that the Gypsies were dirty and had taken over land that didn't belong to them, and their camps were muddy and full of garbage and rusty old cars. Instead it was rather like a little village with modern caravans and late model cars.'

'Nobody was hurt, I hope?' I asked.

'No, not that time, but I didn't want to be part of scaring people. So after that incident I went back to Münster, not only because of that. I wanted to see Aunt Elsa and when I did I realised that she was not well.'

'What was wrong with her?'

'She was old and tired, I think. She'd lived through the war and it had taken its toll. While I was in Germany the group in Groningen petrol-bombed a house and damaged it. Nobody was going to get hurt, Heinrich had always said. "We'll scare them, that's all." Not long after that incident they attacked the house of a Turkish family. You'll have read in the newspapers that a woman and a child died in the fire. I couldn't understand how they could do that. I felt betrayed by the movement. I'd believed we would create a better world by example and through our beliefs, never in such a callous way. So I did not go back to Groningen. I stayed on with Aunt Elsa.'

The waiter was laying the table next to ours. 'I'm sorry,

Kurt. We've been sitting here talking for ages on one cup of coffee. Would you like a Pils?'

'All right,' Kurt said.

'Excellent – waiter!'

He was already at my side. 'Two glasses of Pils and a portion of bitterballen please.'

'Yes, Sir. Right away.'

I wanted to hear more from Kurt. 'Did you manage to get a job in Germany?'

'Yes, I did. I was very lucky to get a job in a bookshop. While I was in prison, I read many books and learned Dutch. I also studied and managed to get my business diploma.'

'That's wonderful. I'm impressed.'

'I took advantage of the opportunities that were there. There wasn't much else to do. I've always loved books and I hope to get a bookshop of my own one day. I was hoping that you could give me some advice on how to go about it.'

'Your Pils, Sir. The bitterballen won't be long.'

'Thank you.' I picked up a cold glass as Kurt did. 'Proost.' We clicked glasses and it felt good. Father and son. We both drank.

'I'll help you all I can, Kurt.'

'Aunt Elsa said you would. She nearly drove me mad. Always saying that I must forgive you and write to you. After all the time that had passed I didn't think that you would have anything to do with me.'

Although I wanted to ask whether he *had* forgiven me, I felt it was not yet the right moment. 'I was very sad when Victor told us that she had passed away. She was a real friend and a wonderful lady.'

'Yes, she was. She made me promise that I would write to you and I did. It was as if she had kept herself alive to hear my promise because soon after that she died suddenly and for the first time in my life I was totally alone. I missed her so much. She was strong and wonderful. I'm sorry I didn't let you know when she died. I should have. I knew how much you liked each other. I couldn't.'

'Your bitterballen, Sir.'

'Thank you. Be careful, Kurt. They'll be hot.'

'All right. Well, now you know all about me. Do you still want to accept me as your son? If you don't, you can blame it all on Victor.'

I laughed, 'Kurt, I feel this is a new beginning. You can live with us for as long as you like and yes, again, I'll help you to realise your ambition.'

I couldn't read his smile. He was pleased, yes, but what was he thinking? Had all thoughts of revenge left him?

I pushed the plate of the fried breadcrumb-covered meaty balls closer to Kurt. 'Help yourself.' Then I watched him take a toothpick and stab one of them rather hard, almost violently, breaking the thin wooden stick.

'Ah.' He looked me in the eye his smile fading. 'I'll try again.'

The pork and veal filling of the bitterballen didn't taste as good as I remembered.

When we finally left the café and walked into my house, Anja and Victor got up from the sofa.

'You took your time,' Anja said to me and looking behind me to Kurt, 'Welcome home, Kurt.'

'Thank you,' he said, 'and thank you too, Victor, for persuading me.'

'That was a pleasure.'

CHAPTER FORTY-FOUR

Life became better than I had dared to hope for. My son was living in my house and seemed to be happy, at least most of the time. Some days I could not reach him. Then he would talk very little and spent most of his free time reading. I would have liked to talk to him then, but thought it unwise to push.

He had found a job in a bookstore in Utrecht, and the owner, Justin van Houten, whom I knew, was pleased with Kurt.

'Very courteous and efficient,' was his verdict.

Kurt and I spent a lot of time together. This perhaps contributed to the realisation that my relationship with Anja was not what it had been. Seeing Kurt every day prompted me to remember Inga. Lovemaking with Anja had become a weekly habit and we both initiated occasional bouts of tension between us that could last for several days.

It was after one of those unpleasant happenings that I decided to go to Terschelling for a week. I needed to get away and what better way than taking off with my cameras and enjoying the fresh air, the clouds and the sky over the sand dunes? When I asked Kurt if he would like to come with me, he said he was too busy in the shop. I was disappointed but also somewhat relieved, as it is not ideal to have someone standing beside you when you want to take a photograph and are waiting for the sun to appear from behind slow moving clouds.

It was evening when I came back to the house a week later, totally refreshed and all unpleasantness forgotten. The house was dark. The first thing I noticed after I entered the hallway was an envelope with Anja's handwriting. I was surprised.

Dearest Piet,
You will hate me. Victor and I have decided that we love each other, so I can no longer stay with you.
Please understand and be happy for us.
Yours always,
Anja

Christ! That's Anja. Be direct. I remembered how she had asked me to be happy for her when she was going to marry Maarten. Shit! She has done it to me again. And Victor. We took him off the street, he took my money and then my woman. But Anja would have been a willing partner if not the instigator. She – . I suddenly felt deadly tired and sat down, the letter still in my hand.

I felt hurt, yet it was not totally unexpected. For some time I had felt that we were both pretending that everything was fine, when it was apparent that it was not. So with the hurt there was also relief at the realization that at last it was all over between Anja and me, and this time for good. I was glad it had ended without any unpleasantness. No yelling, no screaming, no walking in on them in flagrante delicto.

Kurt arrived half an hour later. 'I'm sorry, Father. I did ask Anja to reconsider or at least wait until you were home. I didn't think it fair that she left while you were away. It made me very angry.'

'Fair does not come into it, Kurt. It's okay. It's been coming for some time.'

I was talking as much to myself as to Kurt. I remembered gestures and looks between Anja and Victor, thinking nothing of it at the time. Now they appeared to have been significant. I felt empty. It had been painful when Anja left me for Maarten, but nothing would ever be like the desperate anguish I had felt when Inga left. Anja knew that. It would have made it easier for her to walk out on me this second time.

I looked at my son and wanted to tell him the truth about his uncle's death. Why should I be loyal to Anja after what she had done to me? Was she that sure of me? I considered the consequences again of allowing the truth to come out. It was still not the right time. My son and I were having a relationship despite of what he thought had happened between me and his uncle, I ought to be happy with that.

* * *

Kurt and I fell into an easy domestic routine. I did most of the cooking and showed him, at his insistence, how to work the washing machine. His moods became less frequent and I wondered if Anja had resented Kurt being in the house and he had sensed that.

State of Guilt

Having a pre-dinner drink one evening, I noticed that he was unusually talkative. Obviously there was something that had excited him. Had he met a girl?

'Father,' he said. 'Do you remember how I told you that my dream was one day to have my own bookshop?'

'Yes, of course I do. Have you found an empty shop?'

He shook his head vigorously. 'This is much, much better.'

I laughed at his enthusiasm. 'Come on then, tell me.'

'Well, Mr van Houten is talking about retiring. He's sixty-two and wants to spend the rest of his days practising the flute.'

'I see, and you thought …'

'I did. I can do it.'

'I think you can too. Are you sure that is what you want?'

'More than anything.'

'All right.' I was thinking hard. Why not? Why shouldn't I back him and show him that I had faith in him? 'So are you looking for a partner?'

He nodded. 'A sleeping partner.'

I smiled. 'That's understood.'

'Then you would consider it?'

'Yes, of course I will.'

Kurt got up and came over to me. He put an arm around my shoulder and kissed me on the cheek. Instantly I felt like crying, but I managed to say, almost calmly, 'Let's you and I go and talk to van Houten tomorrow.'

* * *

After consultation with my banker and lawyer, both

of whom urged me to be cautious, I decided to go ahead. The shop had been established for over twenty years, and Kurt's enthusiasm for the book trade plus the fact that he had successfully completed a business course made it appear a worthwhile project, a good deal for all. Kurt would have his own business, I would have close contact with my son and be his partner, and Justin would ease himself into musical retirement.

The official re-opening was a success with healthy sales figures for the day. Van Houten had agreed to stay on as a part time manager for six months. During this period, Kurt would learn whatever he did not yet know about the book trade.

When he came home from that first day of business, he seemed totally pleased with life.

'Justin was surprised that the cookery books did so well.'

'Ah, I'm pleased about that. It was your idea to strengthen that section, wasn't it?'

He relaxed visibly, 'Yes, it was. Cooking and Travel will be a large part of our bread and butter. It doesn't mean that I want to neglect the general mix of titles, such as novels, biographies, reference, and so on but I think I was right in changing the balance.'

As for me, I was extremely happy that I could make some reparation to Kurt for the wrong I felt I had done him. At last the wall I often sensed between us, was hardly there now and I felt that with time its demolition would be complete.